CW00972517

THE ROYAL COURT THEATRE PRESENTS

Instructions for Correct Assembly

by Thomas Eccleshare

Instructions for Correct Assembly was
first performed at the Royal Court Jerwood Theatre
Downstairs, Sloane Square, on Saturday 7 April 2018.

Instructions for Correct Assembly
by Thomas Eccleshare

CAST (in alphabetical order)

Laurie **Michele Austin**
Paul **Jason Barnett**
Harry **Mark Bonnar**
Max **Jane Horrocks**
Amy **Shaniqua Okwok**
Jån/Nick **Brian Vernel**

Director **Hamish Pirie**
Designer **Cai Dyfan**
Lighting Designer **Jack Knowles**
Composer **Duramaney Kamara**
Sound Designer **Helen Skiera**
Movement Director **Vicki Manderson**
Illusionist **Paul Kieve**
Assistant Director **Milli Bhatia**
Casting Director **Amy Ball**
Production Manager **Marius Rønning**
Costume Supervisor **Lucy Walshaw**
Stage Manager **Kate Aisling Jones**
Deputy Stage Manager **Jules Richardson**
Assistant Stage Manager **Kieran Watson**
Stage Management Work Placement **Kara Girvan**
Set built by **Ricky Martin at Ridiculous Solutions**

Instructions for Correct Assembly
by Thomas Eccleshare

Thomas Eccleshare (Writer)

Theatre includes: **Pastoral (& HighTide Festival), I'm Not Here Right Now (Soho); Heather (Tobacco Factory/Bush); 6.0: How Heap... [co-writer] (Dancing Brick).**

Awards include: **Verity Bargate Award; Catherine Johnson Award.**

Thomas is Co-Artistic Director of Dancing Brick.

Michele Austin (Laurie)

For the Royal Court: **Wild Child, The Lost Mariner, Breath, Boom, Been So Long.**

Other theatre includes: **The Seagull (Lyric, Hammersmith); Pride & Prejudice (Crucible, Sheffield); The House That Will Not Stand, The Riots (Tricycle); I Know How I Feel About Eve, Out in the Open (Hampstead); To Kill a Mockingbird (Regent's Park Open Air); Sixty-Six Books (Bush); Generations (Young Vic); The Chain Play (Almeida); 50 Revolutions (Oxford Stage Company); Our Country's Good (Out of Joint); It's a Great Big Shame (Theatre Royal, Stratford East).**

Television includes: **Doctors, EastEnders, The Coroner, The Casual Vacancy, Death in Paradise, Harry & Paul, Holby City, Outnumbered, Peep Show, Silent Witness, Britannia High, Never Better, Secret Life, The Bill, The Wife of Bath, Ugetme, A&E, Gimme Gimme Gimme, Babes in the Wood, Kiss Me Kate, The Perfect Blue.**

Film includes: **The Children Act, What We Did on Our Holiday, Another Year, The Infidel, All or Nothing, Second Nature, Secrets & Lies.**

Jason Barnett (Paul)

For the Royal Court: **Primetime, Friday Night Sex, The Victorian in the Wall, The Girlfriend Experience.**

Other theatre includes: **Saint George & the Dragon, Emil & the Detectives, War Horse, Amato Saltone (National); Life of Galileo, About a Boy (Young Vic); Mogadishu (Lyric, Hammersmith/Royal Exchange, Manchester); The Winter's Tale, Pericles, Days of Significance (RSC); The Fixer (Almeida); Cruisin' (Bush); I Am Mediocre (Work); John Dryden's Tempest (Globe); The 1996 World Cup Final (Schtanhaus/BAC); All the Right People Come Here (Wimbledon Studio).**

Television includes: **Hallmakers, Porride, Bliss, Jonathan Creek, Josh, Agatha Raisin, Death in Paradise, The Javone Prince Show, Bad Education, Phoneshop, Stage Door Johnnies, Doctors, Hotel Trubble, The Legend of Dick & Dom, The Bill, Extras, The Vyvien Vyle Show, Coming of Age, Dead Ringers, Dream Team, Stupid!, Little Britain, Fur TV.**

Film includes: **London Road, Cinderella, Superbob, One Man & His Dog, The Sight, The Reins of Fear.**

Jason is an Associate Artist with Synergy Theatre Project.

Milli Bhatia (Assistant Director)

As assistant director, for the Royal Court: **Girls & Boys.**

As director, theatre includes: **The Hijabi Monologues, My White Best Friend/This Bitter Earth [part of Black Lives Black Words] (Bush); I Have AIDS [Jerwood Assistant Director Programme] (Young Vic); Rats (Duffield Studio, National); EmpowerHouse (Theatre Royal, Stratford East); No Cowboys Only Indians (Courtyard).**

As assistant director, other theatre includes: **Lions & Tigers (Sam Wanamaker Playhouse); Cell Mates, Filthy Business, Luna Gale (Hampstead); The Quiet House (& Park), The Government Inspector (& tour), What Shadows (Birmingham Rep).**

As associate director, other theatre includes: **What If Women Ruled the World? (Manchester International Festival).**

Milli is Trainee Director at the Royal Court. She is an Associate Artist at the Bush Theatre and a Creative Associate at the Gate Theatre.

Mark Bonnar (Harry)

For the Royal Court: **A Girl in a Car with a Man, At the Table, Almost Nothing.**

Other theatre includes: **Queers, The Duchess of Malfi (Old Vic); Sixty-Six Books, Mammals (Bush); The Cherry Orchard (& Oxford Stage Company), Dido Queen of Carthage, Philistines, Cyrano de Bergerac, Anthony & Cleopatra, Flight, Richard III, Chips with Everything (National); Novecento (Trafalgar Studios); Twelfth Night (Wyndham's); Three Sisters, Twelfth Night (Royal Exchange, Manchester); Lost Highway (ENO/Young Vic); Parade (Donmar); Much Ado About Nothing (Salisbury Playhouse); Robin Hood (Caird Co./ NT Loft); Richard III, The Country Wife (Crucible, Sheffield); Out in the Open (Hampstead); Tales from Ovid, Volpone (RSC); The Seal Wife (Wimbledon Attic).**

Television includes: **Urban Myths, Eric Ernie & Me, Humans, Shetland, Porridge, Apple Tree Yard, Unforgotten, Catastrophe, New Blood, Undercover, Jekyll & Hyde, Home Fires, Vera, Midsomer Murders, Grantchester, Line of Duty, Case Histories, The Paradise, Silent Witness, The Minor Character, Twenty Twelve, Doctor Who, Psychoville, Taggart, Phone Shop, Paradox, Pa's, The Bill, Britz, The Trial of Tony Blair, Penkovsky: Nuclear Race, Casualty, Afterlife, Wire in the Blood, The Rainbow Room, Armadillo, Inspector Rebus, The Phoenix & the Carpet.**

Film includes: **Say My Name, The Kid Who Would Be King, Take Down, Sunset Song, X-Moor, Camera Trap.**

Cai Dyfan (Designer)

For the Royal Court: **Violence & Son, Off the Page [Guardian film].**

As designer, other theatre includes: **The Passion, The Village Social (National Theatre Wales); Paul Bunyan (WNO); Sgint, Trwy'r Ddinas Hon (Sherman Cymru); Rhwng Dau Fyd, Chwalfa (Theatr Genedlaethol Cymru); After the End (Dirty Protest); Your Last Breath (Curious Detective); Wasted (Paines Plough/Birmingham Rep/Latitude/tour).**

As associate designer, other theatre includes: **The Lion, the Witch & the Wardrobe (Kensington Gardens); How the Whale Became (ROH); A Life of Galileo (RSC); A Number (Nuffield, Southampton); Mr Burns (Almeida); King Charles III (Almeida/West End); Medea (National).**

As art director, television & film includes: **Convenience, A Discovery of Witches, Hidden/Craith, Born to Kill, Sherlock, Call the Midwife, Hinterland/Y Gwyll, Apostle.**

Jane Horrocks (Max)

For the Royal Court: **Aunt Dan & Lemon, Road.**

Other theatre includes: **Cotton Panic (Manchester International Festival); King Lear (Old Vic); If You Kiss Me Kiss Me, Annie Get Your Gun, The Good Soul of Szechuan (Young Vic); East is East (Trafalgar Studios/tour); Absurd Person Singular, Sweet Panic (West End); Cabaret (Donmar); Macbeth (Greenwich); The Rise & Fall of Little Voice (National/West End).**

Television includes: **Road, Absolutely Fabulous, Never Mind the Horrocks, The Street, Gracie, The Road to Coronation Street, Trollied, Inside No 9.**

Film includes: **The Dressmaker, The Witches, Life is Sweet, Little Voice, Chicken Run, Corpse Bride, Sunshine on Leith, Swimming with Men.**

Duramaney Kamara (Composer)

As music & sound designer, for the Royal Court: **My Mum's a Twat.**

As composer & sound designer, for the Royal Court: **Katzenmusik (Young Court); Tottenham Symphony (Beyond the Court).**

As performer, theatre includes: **Boy (Almeida); The Response (Seagull/Mercury).**

As performer, film includes: **Yardie, What Happened to Evie.**

Paul Kieve (Illusionist)

Theatre includes: **Groundhog Day (& Old Vic), Matilda, Ghost the Musical (& West End), Pippin, Finding Neverland, Side Show (Broadway); The Witches, The Invisible Man, The Lord of the Rings, Zorro (West End); Macbeth (Manchester International Festival).**

Dance includes: **Alice in Wonderland (English National Ballet/Royal Ballet).**

Television includes: **Cranford, Saturday Night Takeaway, Heroes of Magic, BBC History of Magic.**

Film includes: **Harry Potter & the Prisoner of Azkaban, Hugo.**

Live events include: **Dynamo (Seeing is Believing – International tour); David Blaine (2017 American tour); Kate Bush (Before the Dawn – Live Show); Batman Live (World Arena tour); Holiday on Ice (European tour); Mickey & the Magician (Disneyland Paris); Beauty & the Beast (Disney Dream).**

Awards include: **Gold Star Member of the Inner Magic Circle; Creative Fellowship at the Academy of Magical Arts; The Magic Circle Maskelyne Award for Services to British Magic; New York Drama Desk award for Outstanding Set Design (Ghost the Musical).**

Paul has created original effects for over 100 international live productions. His work with Derren Brown includes four West End shows, two television specials and as a consultant on his 'Ghost Train' at Thorpe Park. His book 'Hocus Pocus' has been published in 11 languages. Paul is an Associate Artist at the Old Vic.

Jack Knowles (Lighting Designer)

For the Royal Court: **2071.**

Other theatre includes: **Caroline, or Change (Hampstead/Chichester Festival); Circle Mirror Transformation (Home, Manchester); Wonderland (Nottingham Playhouse); Beginning (National/West End); Barber Shop Chronicles (National/West Yorkshire Playhouse/Australian tour); The Greatest Play in the History of the World, Parliament Square (& Bush), Our Town, Twelfth Night, A Streetcar Named Desire, Wit, The Skriker, There Has Possibly Been An Incident (Royal Exchange, Manchester); Committee (Donmar); 4.48 Psychosis, Reisende auf einem Bein, Happy Days (Schauspielhaus, Hamburg); Junkyard, Pygmalion (Headlong); Winter Solstice (Actors Touring Company); Dan & Phil: The Amazing Tour is Not on Fire (International tour); They Drink it in the Congo, Boy, Carmen Disruption, Game (Almeida); Watership Down (Watermill); The Forbidden Zone (Salzburg Festival/Schaubühne, Berlin/Barbican); Kenny Morgan (Arcola); The Massive Tragedy of Madame Bovary! (Liverpool Everyman/Peepolykus); Cleansed (National); The Haunting of Hill House (Liverpool Playhouse); Phaedra (Enniskillen International Beckett Festival); A Sorrow Beyond Dreams (Burgtheater, Vienna); Lungs, The Yellow Wallpaper (Schaubühne, Berlin); Moth (Hightide/Bush); Say it with Flowers (Hampstead); Night Train (Schauspiel, Köln/Avignon Festival/Theatertreffen Festival, Berlin); In a Pickle (& RSC), Ring-a-Ding-Ding (& Unicorn/New Victory, NYC), Kubla Khan, Land of Lights, Light Show, There Was an Old Woman, The Bounce, Mr & Mrs Moon (Olly Cart).**

Vicki Manderson (Movement Director)

As movement director, for the Royal Court: **a profoundly affectionate, passionate devotion to someone (-noun), The Children.**

As associate movement director, for the Royal Court: **The Twits, Let the Right One In (& National Theatre of Scotland/West End/St Ann's, New York).**

As movement director, other theatre includes: **The Almighty Sometimes (Royal Exchange, Manchester); Cockpit (Royal Lyceum, Edinburgh); We're Still Here (National Theatre Wales); Jimmy's Hall (Abbey, Dublin); 306 (National Theatre of Scotland); See Me Now (Young Vic); Details (Grid Iron); Housed (Old Vic New Voices).**

As associate movement director, other theatre includes: **In Time O' Strife, Black Watch (National Theatre of Scotland); The Curious Incident of the Dog in the Night-Time (National/West End).**

As performer, theatre includes: **In Time O' Strife, Knives in Hens, Beautiful Burnout (& Frantic Assembly), Home Inverness (National Theatre of Scotland); Dr Dee (ENO/Manchester International Festival); The Two Gentlemen of Verona (Royal & Derngate, Northampton); (In)visible dancing, LOL, To the Bone (Protein Dance).**

Shaniqua Okwok (Amy)

Television includes: **Shakespeare & Hathaway – Private Investigators.**

Film includes: **The Crash.**

Awards include: **Doreen Jones Bursary, The Clive Daley Award.**

Instructions for Correct Assembly **is Shaniqua's professional stage debut.**

Hamish Pirie (Director)

For the Royal Court: **Tottenham Symphony (Beyond the Court), Goats, Primetime 2017, Human Animals, Violence & Son, Who Cares, Teh Internet is Serious Business.**

Other theatre includes: **Shibboleth (Abbey, Dublin); I'm With the Band (Traverse/Wales Millennium Centre); Quiz Show, Demos, 50 Plays for Edinburgh (Traverse); Love With a Capital 'L', 3 Seconds, Most Favoured, The Last Bloom (Traverse/Òran Mór); Bravo Figaro (Royal Opera House/Traverse); Salt Root & Roe (Donmar/ Trafalgar Studios); Stacy (& Trafalgar Studios), Purgatory (Arcola); Pennies (nabokov); Paper House (Flight 5065).**

Hamish trained as Resident Assistant Director at Paines Plough and at the Donmar Warehouse. He was previously Associate Director at the Traverse Theatre. Hamish is an Associate Director at the Royal Court.

Helen Skiera (Sound Designer)

For the Royal Court: **Bodies, Adler & Gibb [as associate].**

As sound designer, other theatre includes: **Betrayal, Echo's End, The Magna Carta Plays (Salisbury Playhouse); House & Garden (Watermill); Good Dog, I know all the secrets in my world, The Legend of Hamba, The Epic Adventure of Nhamo the Manyika Warrior (Tiata Fahodzi/Watford Palace); Here I Belong (Pentabus); The Encounter (Complicite); Harajuku Girls (Finborough); The Dog the Night & the Knife, Pandora's Box, Miss Julie (Arcola); The Boy Who Climbed Out of His Face (Shunt); Last Words You'll Hear (Almeida); Advice for the Young at Heart (Theatre Centre); The Centre (Islington Community Theatre); The Criminals, House of Bones, Medea, Colors (Drama Centre); Concrete Jungle (Riverside); The Riot Act, Beautiful Blows (Mayhem Company).**

As associate sound designer, other theatre includes: **Barbershop Chronicles (National); Cat On a Hot Tin Roof (Young Vic/West End); I'd Rather Goya Robbed Me of My Sleep Than Some Other Arsehole (Gate).**

As musician, television includes: **Right Said Fred – Celebrity Big Brother Live performance.**

Brian Vernel (Jån/Nick)

Theatre includes: **The Seagull (Lyric, Hammersmith); Certain Young Men – Queer Theatre (National); Barbarians (Young Vic); Future Conditional (Old Vic); Takin' Over the Asylum (Royal Lyceum, Edinburgh/Citizens); Four Parts Broken (National Theatre of Scotland/Traverse).**

Television includes: **Collateral, The Tunnel, Doctor Who, The Missing, The Last Kingdom, The Casual Vacancy, Grantchester, Prey, The Field of Blood.**

Film includes: **Dunkirk, Star Wars: The Force Awakens, Winter Song, Offender, Let Us Prey.**

THE ROYAL COURT THEATRE

The Royal Court Theatre is the writers' theatre. It is a leading force in world theatre for energetically cultivating writers – undiscovered, emerging and established.

Through the writers, the Royal Court is at the forefront of creating restless, alert, provocative theatre about now. We open our doors to the unheard voices and free thinkers that, through their writing, change our way of seeing.

Over 120,000 people visit the Royal Court in Sloane Square, London, each year and many thousands more see our work elsewhere through transfers to the West End and New York, UK and international tours, digital platforms, our residencies across London, and our site-specific work. Through all our work we strive to inspire audiences and influence future writers with radical thinking and provocative discussion.

The Royal Court's extensive development activity encompasses a diverse range of writers and artists and includes an ongoing programme of writers' attachments, readings, workshops and playwriting groups. Twenty years of the International Department's pioneering work around the world means the Royal Court has relationships with writers on every continent.

Within the past sixty years, John Osborne, Samuel Beckett, Arnold Wesker, Ann Jellicoe, Howard Brenton and David Hare have started their careers at the Court. Many others including Caryl Churchill, Athol Fugard, Mark Ravenhill, Simon Stephens, debbie tucker green, Sarah Kane – and, more recently, Lucy Kirkwood, Nick Payne, Penelope Skinner and Alistair McDowall – have followed.

The Royal Court has produced many iconic plays from Laura Wade's **Posh** to Jez Butterworth's **Jerusalem** and Martin McDonagh's **Hangmen**.

Royal Court plays from every decade are now performed on stage and taught in classrooms and universities across the globe.

It is because of this commitment to the writer that we believe there is no more important theatre in the world than the Royal Court.

Supported using public funding by
ARTS COUNCIL ENGLAND

ROYAL

COMING UP AT THE ROYAL COURT

18 Apr – 2 Jun

The Prudes
By Anthony Neilson

13 Jun – 23 Jun

Notes From the Field
By Anna Deavere Smith
Presented by LIFT and the Royal Court Theatre with support from Jordan Roth.

20 Jun – 11 Aug

One For Sorrow
By Cordelia Lynn

12 Jul – 11 Aug

Pity
By Rory Mullarkey

5 Sep – 13 Oct

The Woods
By Robert Alan Evans

21 Sep – 6 Oct

Debris Stevenson
Co-commissioned by 14–18 NOW and the Royal Court Theatre, supported by Jerwood Charitable Foundation, in association with Nottingham Playhouse and Leicester Curve.

25 Oct – 24 Nov

ear for eye
By debbie tucker green
Produced in association with Barbara Broccoli.

28 Nov – 12 Jan

Hole
By Ellie Kendrick
Part of the Royal Court's Jerwood New Playwrights programme, supported by Jerwood Charitable Foundation.

6 Dec – 26 Jan

The Cane
By Mark Ravenhill

Tickets from £12

royalcourttheatre.com

Sloane Square London, SW1W 8AS ⊖ Sloane Square
⇌ Victoria Station 🐦 royalcourt 📘 royalcourttheatre

Supported using public funding by
ARTS COUNCIL ENGLAND

JERWOOD CHARITABLE FOUNDATION

ROYAL COURT SUPPORTERS

The Royal Court is a registered charity and not-for-profit company. We need to raise £1.5 million every year in addition to our core grant from the Arts Council and our ticket income to achieve what we do.

We have significant and longstanding relationships with many generous organisations and individuals who provide vital support. Royal Court supporters enable us to remain the writers' theatre, find stories from everywhere and create theatre for everyone.

We can't do it without you.

PUBLIC FUNDING

Arts Council England, London
British Council

TRUSTS & FOUNDATIONS

The Backstage Trust
The Bryan Adams Charitable Trust
The Austin & Hope Pilkington Trust
Martin Bowley Charitable Trust
Gerald Chapman Fund
CHK Charities
The City Bridge Trust
The Clifford Chance Foundation
Cockayne - Grants for the Arts
The Nöel Coward Foundation
Cowley Charitable Trust
The Eranda Rothschild Foundation
Lady Antonia Fraser for The Pinter Commission
Genesis Foundation
The Golden Bottle Trust
The Haberdashers' Company
The Paul Hamlyn Foundation
Roderick & Elizabeth Jack
Jerwood Charitable Foundation
Kirsh Foundation
The Mackintosh Foundation
The Andrew Lloyd Webber Foundation
The London Community Foundation

John Lyon's Charity
Clare McIntyre's Bursary
The Andrew W. Mellon Foundation
The David & Elaine Potter Foundation
The Richard Radcliffe Charitable Trust
Rose Foundation
Royal Victoria Hall Foundation
The Sackler Trust
The Sobell Foundation
John Thaw Foundation
The Wellcome Trust
The Garfield Weston Foundation

CORPORATE SPONSORS

Aqua Financial Solutions Ltd
Bloomberg
Cadogan Estates
Colbert
Edwardian Hotels, London
Fever-Tree
Gedye & Sons
Kirkland & Ellis International LLP
Kudos
MAC
Room One
Sister Pictures
Sky Drama

CORPORATE MEMBERS

Auerbach & Steele Opticians
CNC – Communications & Network Consulting
Cream
Left Bank Pictures
Rockspring Property Investment Managers
Tetragon Financial Group

For more information or to become a foundation or business supporter contact Camilla Start: camillastart@royalcourttheatre.com/020 7565 5064.

Supported using public funding by
ARTS COUNCIL ENGLAND

"There are no spaces, no rooms in my opinion, with a greater legacy of fearlessness, truth and clarity than this space."

Simon Stephens, Associate Playwright

Royal Court invests in the future of the theatre, offering writers the support, time and resources to find their voices and tell their stories, asking the big questions and responding to the issues of the moment.

As a registered charity, the Royal Court relies on the generous support of individuals to seek out, develop and nurture new voices. Please join us in **Writing The Future** by donating today.

You can donate online at royalcourttheatre.com/donate or via our donation box in the Bar & Kitchen.

We can't do it without you.

To find out more about the different ways in which you can be involved please contact Charlotte Cole on 020 7565 5049 / charlottecole@royalcourttheatre.com

Thomas Eccleshare

INSTRUCTIONS
FOR CORRECT ASSEMBLY

OBERON BOOKS
LONDON

WWW.OBERONBOOKS.COM

First published in 2018 by Oberon Books Ltd
521 Caledonian Road, London N7 9RH
Tel: +44 (0) 20 7607 3637 / Fax: +44 (0) 20 7607 3629
e-mail: info@oberonbooks.com
www.oberonbooks.com

A catalogue record for this book is available from the British Library.

PB ISBN: 9781786824974
E ISBN: 9781786824967

Cover image: Root.

Printed and bound by 4edge Limited, Essex, UK.
eBook conversion by CPI Group (UK) Ltd, Croydon, CR0 4YY.

For my parents.

Characters

MAX, *around 50*
HARI, *around 50*
JÅN / NICK, *18-20*
LAURIE, *around 50*
PAUL, *around 50*
AMY, *18*

Place

The rooms of a neat family home. It could almost be a catalogue.

A note on Jån and Nick

In my mind Nick and Jån are played by the same actor, so to all intents and purposes are identical. As a result at times there may a tension, even confusion, about who we are watching.

1

Kitchen

MAX	Did you find what you were looking for?
HARI	Yes I did. Lovely girl helped me in the shop. She pointed me in the right direction.
MAX	Oh good.
HARI	On the way out I noticed they had a special offer. A do it yourself type thing.
MAX	You like those.
HARI	Exactly. It's not much of a commitment financially speaking and might be a bit of fun.
MAX	Sounds good.
HARI	I thought we could have a go at it together, you know like we did with the upstairs bed?
MAX	Oh I enjoyed that.
HARI	You had natural flat pack talent.
MAX	You said I was the Susan Boyle of DIY.
HARI	This might be a little more complicated than the bed but still, I'm sure it's the kind of thing we can crack on our own.
MAX	Is it in the hall then or
HARI	No. It contains some special components or something so they send it out direct.
MAX	Well I'll look forward to that.

Garage

HARI and MAX stand surrounded by parts. A chaos of bits and pieces. HARI is looking at a page in an inch-thick book of instructions. MAX is trying to peek at it too. They read intently, very confused.

MAX   Can I have a

HARI   One second.

Silence.

MAX   Just a quick look

HARI   One second love stop breaking my concentration.

Silence. HARI peers at the book as if the distance he's reading it from will make a difference. MAX opens her mouth to speak. Then closes it. Silence.

HARI holds the book out for her to take. She takes it. She turns to the first page.

MAX   One: check you have all of the component parts. Two: take the laminate frame (left) and place it on its plastic neoprene base, upright. Twist two of the fiddly ones into the pre-drilled holes in the heel.

HARI   These?

MAX   Yes. Two. Attach the toe mouldings to the tops of the fiddly ones and screw.

HARI   What do you mean the top?

MAX   The top. I'm just trying to describe the drawing.

He does it. It looks good.

MAX   Hey how about that.

HARI   Well that's the beauty of it. It's all these separate parts. They come in bits. They're scattered all over the floor. You're looking at them and thinking okay this doesn't make any sense how will this ever fit together and be our new bed or desk or whatnot and I wouldn't have thought that that went there or in that order but then two hours later once it's all come together you're looking at it and thinking: wow.

Study

HARI is on the phone.

HARI   Well I'm struggling to see why I pay for next day delivery if it's not guaranteed. Yes that's the whole reason I signed up for the prime service. Yes also for the ad-free access to the premium music library and the original video content. I've started season one but I didn't get into it if I'm honest. Did you think? I thought it was a bit too complex for its own good actually. Yes sort of never bought into the concei – Look this is totally off the subject. I paid for something perfect. I don't think it's too much to ask to be delivered something perfect. There are some missing components and I need them sent out as soon as possible. Some ball bearings, some stainless steel six pins. And well I've got a list: Ball bearings, chrome, 5; Six pins, stainless steel, 2; Circuit board, 1; Glass eye, grey-green, 1; Wig, Chestnut, 1; Toenails, 3, left big, right third, right pinky; Last one, lithium batteries.

Pause.

Thank you.

<u>Garage</u>

HARI and MAX are surrounded by parts, working to fit two pieces of plastic together.

MAX	I have to say I think it's very clever all these things. I mean it's a faff putting it all together and when you lose a bit and the staff can be annoying but when it works it is very good.
HARI	I think they're an excellent company.
MAX	What they've done is take the real expense of the work
HARI	The manpower
MAX	Out of the equation
HARI	Exactly
MAX	And said, okay, here's all the stuff, but wouldn't you rather do it yourself than have some guy in a factory
HARI	Who's more expensive
MAX	Who's more expensive anyway
HARI	Or in a factory in India or something
MAX	Which is immoral and gone well go on then off you go have a good Sunday and give us a call if you get stuck.
HARI	Which you're very welcome to do.
MAX	Like we did with the wardrobe.
HARI	Yes although that was their fault.
MAX	Why because you put the drawers in upside down?
HARI	The instructions were vague.

They continue to work.

MAX	I had an email from Jenny. They're all visiting Fi in Hong Kong.
HARI	Gap year?

MAX	Yes, she's got an internship apparently. She said over 400 people applied.
HARI	Wow. Clever girl.
MAX	Yes. Have you got the Phillips?
HARI	Toolbox.
MAX	And did you see Jeanette reposted an article her son wrote for a magazine which looks very good.
HARI	Gosh he's done well if he's writing for a magazine.
MAX	I'd not heard of it before but Jeanette's post said you can get it in shops you know it's not just online.
HARI	Impressive.
	They are making progress.
MAX	Hey you'll never guess who just did my eyes at the hospital.
HARI	Dr. Safani wasn't there?
MAX	No there was a junior doctor. Milo Hooper.
HARI	You're kidding. He can't be old enough to drive.
MAX	He still looks about twelve.
HARI	So he's a doctor?
MAX	I know.
HARI	I remember when he and Nick got suspended together.
MAX	And Jill gave me hell as if it was my fault.
HARI	I'll say now what I said at the time: if he wasn't involved then why was he holding the can of Lynx.
	Pause.
HARI	A doctor.
MAX	I know.
HARI	Wow.

Pause.

HARI   Good on him.

MAX   Absolutely.

HARI   Jill must be chuffed.

MAX nods. She holds up what she's been working on: it looks like the perfect plastic arm of a male manikin. They look at each other, and smile.

Living Room

HARI stands opposite JÅN, a boy of about eighteen.

Silence.

He stares at JÅN, who stares back, impassive.

HARI   Well?

              Silence.

HARI   Are you going to say something?

              Pause.

HARI   Anything?

              Pause.

HARI   Great.

              HARI leaves the room. JÅN stands in silence.

              HARI returns carrying a toolbox. He removes a screwdriver from the toolbox. He goes to JÅN. He unscrews the back of JÅN's head and removes it. He presses something. He pulls out a cluster of wires and circuitry. He finds a particular wire and looks at it. He sighs. He cuts the wire. He replaces the back of JÅN's head. He stands back from him again and presses a button on a shiny remote control.

JÅN   Hello.

HARI   That's better.

Conservatory

HARI, MAX, PAUL and LAURIE are having a pre-dinner drink.

LAURIE   We honestly couldn't believe it. Paul picked up the
              phone and as soon as I heard her voice I thought:
              this is going to be good news. Whenever she has bad
              news she waits for us to call. Or worse, we get a call
              from Minty, that's Ames's best friend – absolutely
              brilliant painter actually we went to one of her shows
              last term and she really is exceptionally talented –
              anyway she'll call and it's all oh Laurie there's been a
              disaster, we've missed the last train can you come and
              pick us up from some nightclub or other we've been
              having too good a time. Anyway this time it's Ames
              on the phone and I just grabbed it off Paul – I wasn't
              going to let him have all the fun – he got the AS's, I
              got the GCSE's so it was my turn – and bless her: she
              was crying. Tears of joy. Three A stars and an A, and
              to be honest I think the chemistry department is total
              rubbish at that school so at any normal school I think
              it might even have been four A stars. So she's off to
              Oxford at the end of the month.

HARI   To Amy!

Dining Room

HARI, MAX, PAUL and LAURIE are in the middle of dinner.

PAUL   You wouldn't believe the amount of work they have
              to do. I mean I try not to get too involved but I
              had to have a word with the coach I said Phil these
              are fourteen year old kids, you know, they've got
              homework, they've got social lives, Callum has this

girl he's trying to lose his virginity to – oh come on I'm only joking – but you take my point, they can't be in every morning at six smashing lengths before school. It's taking the joy out of it. Cal used to love swimming, he'd take it seriously of course, you have to if you're at his level, but he used to do it because he enjoyed it. With these national squads it's just work work work; they treat them like they're professional athletes. I said come on Phil give him the weekend off let him go on this date or whatever. And you know what he said to me he said: when Callum's got an Olympic medal round his neck, he'll have all the pussy he wants.

They all laugh.

HARI   To Callum!

Sitting Room

HARI, MAX, PAUL and LAURIE are having an after-dinner coffee.

LAURIE   I'm actually genuinely concerned. Paul will tell you that I've been having trouble sleeping because of it. Tossing and turning and just trying to think how best to handle it. I mean, what kind of pressure does it put on a child to be told you're an actual genuine prodigy? At architecture. At eleven years old. I mean how can they know? Of course these tests are evaluated by RIBA so it's all legit but still, when her form teacher's looking me in the eye and saying that in twenty years time Sophia will be the next Zaha Hadid what are you supposed to say?

MAX   It's fucking ridiculous.

HARI   To Sophia!

14

Kitchen

MAX and LAURIE are clearing up.

LAURIE	Ames sends her love by the way.
MAX	Oh that's kind, send it back.
LAURIE	She was so upset she couldn't get down for the funeral.
MAX	Oh god I didn't even think about it.
LAURIE	It was just you know because she'd already been signed up and it was abroad you know not just a day trip or whatever and I think it counted towards her coursework so.
MAX	Honestly I wouldn't have wanted her to cancel. It's great she's so focussed.
LAURIE	She said she'd sent a card?
MAX	Yes. It was very sweet.
LAURIE	Well that's good that's polite.

MAX nods. They wash.

LAURIE	Also because it was booked through the school I think that was another reason they couldn't cancel it or something. I just don't want you to think that she was being rude.
MAX	No, I don't.

They wash a bit. Silence.

LAURIE	And how are you both doing?
MAX	We're good. We're good.
LAURIE	Good.

They wash.

MAX	It can happen to anyone that's what's so terrifying.
LAURIE	Of course it can.

15

Pause.

MAX   It's not anything you've done or that anyone's done it's just

LAURIE   No, quite, quite.

MAX   You know Amy or Callum or Sophia. You know?

LAURIE   Mm.

MAX   Could have been.

LAURIE   Mm could have been.

MAX   It's just well you just don't know.

LAURIE   No.

MAX   No.

LAURIE   No.

MAX   No.

LAURIE   No.

They wash up.

LAURIE   That lamb was really terrific by the way. You put me to shame.

Garage

PAUL and HARI are admiring JAN.

HARI   You can touch him if you like.

        PAUL approaches and begins to have a root around.

HARI   The really clever thing it does actually come here you'll like this. If you want to tell it a story about yourself, you know some goal you once scored or thing you did that was really cool. Well if you programme it right he'll remember all that stuff and

	upload it to the cloud so you've got a sort of walking sort of legacy.
PAUL	Sweet.
HARI	Of course they're a bit more unreliable the flatpack ones
PAUL	That's the price you pay
HARI	But I invested a little extra to get a call out helpline so if anything does go wrong – simple.
PAUL	Speaking of money, Hari.
HARI	Have a feel here. I mean you expect a little give and take around the jointing but this is practically invisible. Go on have a real feel.

PAUL strokes JAN's face.

PAUL	Ooh yeah. That is lovely. What's the traction control like?
HARI	Oh he'll go anywhere – alright Paul. *(PAUL stops stroking.)* We haven't done it yet but I've seen a tutorial on YouTube take him mountain biking.
PAUL	Get out.
HARI	Seriously. He's got PLS palm grip, and Double Knuckle Cladding on every finger so should be able to hold on to just about anything you throw at him.

PAUL's got his head to JAN's chest.

PAUL	Nice growly base notes coming from there.
HARI	Oh there's some pretty serious punch under the hood. The truth is most of this is just casing. The real processing power's on a chip that sticks to the back here look.
PAUL	Quite versatile then.

HARI	Oh completely. In theory with a good scalpel and some anaesthetic there's no real reason you couldn't fit it to a I don't know a cat.
PAUL	Maybe I'll fit one to the wife. Might be the only way I can get her to tidy her tennis stuff away! And what you train him up do you? Try to give him a grounded moral framework based on viewing your actions and the actions of people within his environment from which he begins to interpret the social norms of the locale in which he's been placed?
HARI	Yup. I'm also doing quite a lot with the remote control.
PAUL	And dare I approach the thorny issue of cost?
HARI	I mean it's an outlay of course it is. But once you're paying monthly and you think about the premium nature of the product and what it can do. Really not that bad at all.
PAUL	Speaking of money, Hari
HARI	The height's generous.
PAUL	Just would be good to have a chat about
HARI	Good options on eye and hair colour.
PAUL	You know not rushing just to get an idea of
HARI	Yeah no of course. I've spoken to the bank. I should have the bulk with you by the end of the year.
PAUL	Great.
HARI	We really do appreciate it so much.
PAUL	I know you do. That's not why I'm
HARI	No I know
PAUL	It's just, cos we're saving up for the loft so
	Pause.
PAUL	Poor Nick.

HARI	Yeah.

Silence. They look at JAN again.

PAUL	So when do we get a chance to meet him?

Kitchen

MAX	When?
HARI	The fourteenth. Here let me do all this you made dinner.
MAX	Oh Hari.
HARI	What was I supposed to do he was interested?
MAX	It's just pressure that's all. I don't want
HARI	What they're our friends!
MAX	I know but
HARI	There that's on eco-wash – done by the time we wake up.
MAX	We haven't even met him ourselves yet.
HARI	They just want to come round and see him. He'll impress them. Believe me.
MAX	*(Imploring.)* Please. What if he's embarrassing or we can't get him to behave or
HARI	Oh come on it doesn't matter. They'll just come round, meet him, be impressed, then leave, what's so scary about that?
MAX	Please Hari. I'd just rather not.

Pause. HARI sighs.

HARI	Alright. I'll text Paul and make an excuse.
MAX	Thank you.

Hallway

HARI	Cab's here!
NICK	*(Off)* Coming!
	NICK enters. He looks identical to JAN.
MAX	Got everything?
NICK	Yes Mum.
HARI	Need a hand with anything?
NICK	I think I'm good. See you guys.
HARI	'See you guys' listen to him as if he's popping to the shops.
NICK	I'm gonna see you in a few weeks. It's not a big deal, is it?
MAX	Er our big grown up boy is going to university and one day he's going to be a big grown up man and time goes past very quickly and I'm your soppy old mum so yes it's a big deal!
NICK	Alright alright.
HARI	You look very smart mate.
NICK	Cheers Dad.
MAX	You've got your bag?
NICK	Er no I thought I might actually leave my bag.
HARI	I see you've packed your cheek.
MAX	What would he do without it?
NICK	Guys I've got to go.
MUM	You've got your admissions letter.
NICK	Mum it's online you don't need to bring it.
HARI	Passport?
NICK	Dad
HARI	Careful with your passport

MAX and NICK "It's the most valuable thing you own"

HARI	It is! And remember when you get your room – first thing you check?
NICK	That the shelves have been put up right.
MAX	Hari what kind of
HARI	It happened to a friend of mine in our first term. Bang, knocked out cold by an Oxford Dictionary of Quotations.
NICK	Sorry Mum.
MAX	Sorry for what?
NICK	That I'm leaving you alone with him, you going to be okay?
HARI	*(Cuffing him playfully.)* Maybe you should leave some of that cheek at home eh?
MAX	So you'll call us when you get settled in won't you?
NICK	Course.
MAX	And you're definitely going to try to quit smoking?
NICK	Mum.
HARI	Good luck mate – knock 'em dead.
NICK	Will do.
	He picks up his bags.
NICK	Well
MAX	Well
NICK	Gis a hug then.

2

Garage

MAX is reading from the instructions. HARI is fiddling with JÅN who is inanimate.

HARI   Read it out for me.

MAX   Okay. So. In order to setup an SD card with a newly built version of SON you will need to: 1. Format the selected SON persona into the /output as BORN. 2. Copy onto

HARI   Hang on hang on. And. There.

JÅN wakes up, enthusiastically.

JÅN   Don't tell me this is my room? Honey I love it! OMG it's literally perfect I'm like having a literal heart attack right now. The poured concrete, the garage doors, the full sized car accessory it's like 'mechanic-chic' or something, it's gorgeous, it's cheeky.

MAX   Maybe turn down the 'opinionated' dial?

JÅN   Did you guys do this damp wall? It is out of this world I'm going crazy here!

HARI   Definitely.

HARI fiddles with something on the back of JÅN's head.

JÅN   I love how you've just like scattered shammy cloths everywhere. Seriously it's like you've taken a Pinterest of like my dream room and just like built it.

HARI   Okay let's try this!

HARI presses something.

JÅN   Oh. My. Days. Is this my room?

HARI   Oops, I think I turned it the wrong way.

JÅN   Bitch what was you thinking? These walls are like puke coloured or some shit. What you walked into Homebase and was like here give me a paint that looks like I done a shit on a hangover.

MAX	Come on Hari.
HARI	Right you are. Ah, I think I've found the Sassy guage. I'll just take it right down shall I?
JÅN	And I'm sorry yeah but this door fuck me are you cunts blind or something?!
MAX	Right down.
HARI	Here we go.

JÅN switches to a meekness bordering on psycopathic.

MAX	Jån?

JÅN looks at MAX.

MAX	Jån?
JÅN	*(Monotone.)* You have pretty eyes.
MAX	Er, okay.

JÅN looks MAX up and down, studying every inch of the skin on her face.

JÅN	And your skin is lovely.
HARI	I might just split the difference.
MAX	Do.
JÅN	Could I see your teeth?

HARI makes another change and JÅN switches to a confident, polite, eighteen-year-old boy.

JÅN	Hi.
MAX	That looks better.
JÅN	Is this where I'll be sleeping? It's nice.
MAX	Much better.
JÅN	It's great to finally meet you both properly.

They look at him, and smile.

TV Room

HARI and MAX are refitting parts of JĀN. His body parts are in pieces around the room. His head rests on the side. The TV is on and they half-watch as they work. HARI is screwing some circuitry in a leg. MAX begins to cut down the flesh of an arm, consulting the instructions at all times.

HARI	Have you seen the left shin?
MAX	It's round here somewhere.
HARI	I was polishing it earlier before I had a go on his nostrils.
MAX	Is this it?
HARI	That's a buttock, Max.
MAX	Oh.
HARI	Honestly we'll end up with the bloody elephant man with you in charge.
MAX	I knew we shouldn't have done it inside.
HARI	I wanted to watch out for Katherine she's supposed to be in this one.
MAX	Sort of could be a shin.
HARI	Ah here we are; in with the toes and feet. I thought I said
MAX	Sorry sorry
HARI	I'm not having a go but otherwise things'll get lost and you only notice you're missing a piece when it's too la – ooh ooh!
MAX	Is that her?
HARI	Yes.
MAX	No.
HARI	Yes!
MAX	Gosh she's grown up.

HARI	Wow.
MAX	She's very good.
HARI	Intense!
MAX	Yes.
HARI	Sexy!
MAX	Alright Hari.
HARI	Sorry.
MAX	Ooh watch out Katherine I don't like the look of that storage room one bit.
HARI	Haven't you been reading the papers there's a bloody killer on the loose?
MAX	Well don't go in on your own.
HARI	You sexy idiot! Ah!
MAX	Eurgh!

They watch her get killed. A pause for breath.

HARI	Very good. She was always talented.
MAX	I should text Fran and say we saw her.

HARI takes the shin over and begins screwing it into the knee. They work a little in silence.

MAX   You know – you'll think I'm soppy – but, sometimes, I think my favourite times with Nick were just those, were just you know those schoolnights not doing anything. Like we could go on holiday or maybe out for a meal for someone's birthday and it was lovely of course it was but somehow, I don't know, it *had* to be lovely if that makes sense? Whereas some nights, when the three of us were just, maybe, like this, watching TV together, the kind of night you'll forget about ninety-nine times out of a hundred. But we'd be all sitting there and just, watching you know and, yeah, I don't know, you'd be half-reading

26

the newspaper, Nick'd be texting or on whatsapp or whatever the latest thing is or doodling a tattoo on his arm and yeah it was just nice, you know?

Pause.

MAX Have you got an elbow lying around by any chance?

HARI Oh sorry yes, I was using it as a paperweight.

Dining Room

MAX, HARI and JÅN are eating dinner. JÅN is playing with his food. MAX nods at HARI and HARI taps JÅN on the shoulder. JÅN stops playing with his food.

MAX Shall we tell our days?

HARI Oh yes.

MAX Jån?

JÅN Yes please.

HARI Right I'll go. I went to school. Had a good day actually. Got some jip from year 13 but had a nice lunch. I popped round to Al's on the way home too, which was nice. He said I could help myself to his old washing machine if I fancied it. I thought I might take the motor out and have a fiddle around. I'm sure there'd be some good parts in there. Max?

MAX I had a lovely day. I met Carla before work which was really nice. She's thinking of going back to work, now all the kids are at school.

HARI That's a good idea.

MAX Work was good. They're trying to get me to train up the new boy in Kitchenware so he can take off some of my workload which will be excellent.

HARI It's not fair the way they work you.

MAX	So hopefully this can be a way of getting some of my life back. Then I went to yoga and had a really good sweat.
HARI	We're eating love.
MAX	How about you Jån? What did you do?
JÅN	*(Talking with his mouth open and full of food.)* I cleaned my room.
HARI	Jån?
JÅN	Sorry. *(Still open and still full of food.)* I cleaned my room thoroughly.
	MAX and HARI look at each other. MAX nods. HARI takes out the remote and taps on it a few times. Beep!
MAX	What did you do again Jån?
	He swallows the food, but mumbles monosyllabically into his chest with his head down like a sulky teenager.
JÅN	Clned m'room.
HARI	It's okay it's okay.
	HARI fiddles with the remote again and nods at MAX.
MAX	Jån?
	JÅN now talks eagerly and clearly looking each of them in the eye in turn.
JÅN	I cleaned my room from top to bottom, it took ages but was worth it as now I have everything just the way I like it.
MAX	Good boy. What else?
JÅN	I ate a nice lunch.
MAX	What did you have for lunch?
JÅN	I had a sandwich of bread and cheese and swimming.
	Beat.

HARI	Again.
JÅN	A sandwich of bread and cheese and swimming.
HARI	Of bread?
JÅN	And swimming swimming.

MAX and HARI glance at each other.

JÅN	Swimming swimming swimming swimming swimming.

HARI gets up and fiddles with the back of JÅN's head. He returns to his seat and taps on the remote.

HARI	Again.
JÅN	A sandwich of bread and cheese and ham.
MAX	Yum yum.
JÅN	Then I watched some television. A comedy show about some hilarious poofs who

HARI taps the remote. Beep.

JÅN	A comedy show about some hilarious queer

Beep.

JÅN	About some hilarious gay

Beep.

JÅN	Some hilarious people. It was really good. I liked it because they smack each other over the head the whole time and there's a guy in it who always ends up with his face in the mud. It makes me laugh so much.

Pause. MAX nods. HARI fiddles again.

JÅN	I like the show so much because the people in it are so stupid they're always doing stupid things.

Pause. HARI fiddles again.

JÅN	I don't really like the show though. I think the way it portrays the characters is patronising to be honest.

MAX	In what way?
JÅN	They have no opinions of their own. They just fall over or get banged on the head and stuff. It's supposed to be funny.
MAX	Well it sounds a bit silly to me.
JÅN	Then I made myself a cup of tea.
MAX	Mmmmm.
JÅN	A really fucking strong one. Not that grey milky shit Max sometimes slops up.
	Beep.
JÅN	A nice strong one, much better than Max's.
	Beep.
JÅN	But I couldn't get it quite how Max does it unfortunately.
MAX	Practice makes perfect.
JÅN	I'll have to keep a better eye on you!
MAX	Haha exactly.
HARI	It's nice to just put your feet up with a cup of tea sometimes isn't it?
JÅN	Fuck yeah! *(Beep.)* Hell yes! *(Beep.)* When you feel it's well earned.
HARI	Quite.
JÅN	I took the tea outside I hope you don't mind.
MAX	Of course – it's your house too.
JÅN	Just into the conservatory. It's nice being amongst all the flowers.
HARI	Isn't it.
MAX	A little piece of heaven I sometimes think.
JÅN	There's no such thing as heaven.

HARI pauses over the remote. He and MAX have a look at each other. They let it go.

JÅN   And I sat with my tea and had a read of the paper on Hari's computer. Hope you don't mind Hari.

HARI   Anything interesting?

JÅN   Some stuff about immigration. Everyone seems up in arms one way or the other.

HARI   It's a complex problem.

JÅN   Dunno, seems simple enough to me. England should stay English what's so complex about that? There are parts of Birmingham that have Erdu street signs.

HARI   Well

Beep.

JÅN   I just think the middle class totally disregard the genuine fear of the working man that lower paid jobs are being taken by cheaper immigrant workers and traditional white working class communities are being broken up.

Beep.

JÅN   All international borders are illogical constructs that have more to do with a self-perpetuating oligarchy of rich capitalists than any actual concern for culture or the welfare of the people.

Beep.

JÅN   The way the papers twist the immigration issue is, to be honest, offensive. Modern Britain is multicultural, that's what makes us who we are, that's what makes us successful. Look at Mo Farah. If we didn't allow skilled immigrants into the country the NHS for one would totally collapse and that's supposed to be our crown jewel.

MAX   Look at nursing.

JÅN	Exactly, the nursing profession is propped up by skilled immigrant workers.
HARI	Not to mention art, culture
JÅN	The whole idea of traditional Britishness is fake anyway, we've always been a tapestry of influences.
MAX	I couldn't agree more.
JÅN	Anyway then I got bored of the paper so I went on the internet and had an incredible wank to some really filthy stuff I found *(Beep.)* To a google image search of Katy Perry. *(Beep.)* Did some homework in my room for half an hour. An essay about the objectification of women in the modern media.
MAX	Sounds like a very productive day.
JÅN	Then I went outside for a bit.
MAX	Oh.
HARI	Hmm.
MAX	I'm not sure how we feel about that.
JÅN	Just down to the corner shop.
MAX	Right?
JÅN	I bought a packet of fags. Came back here and had them in the garden. They were lovely; really moreish. Ended up just smoking one after the other.
	MAX and HARI look at each other. Beep. JÅN goes to sleep. Silence.
HARI	Getting there.
MAX	Yes.
HARI	I'll have a look in the instructions about those cigarettes. Just a bit of rewiring needed I expect.
	Pause.
HARI	This is delicious by the way.

Kitchen

NICK	So
HARI	Hi.
NICK	Hi.
HARI	Your mum's in bed.
NICK	Well it's late so.
HARI	Yeah.

Silence.

HARI	Do you want anything? A cup of tea? Or I could warm you something up. We had some lasagne, there's some lasagne in the fridge if you fancy.
NICK	I'm good. I ate at the station.
HARI	Great. Yeah some good options at the station. There's a Pret I think even now did you see that I mean I know you know that's probably not your

Silence.

HARI	Anyway.

Pause.

HARI	I won't wake Mum if you don't mind. She's been having trouble sleeping anyway so.
NICK	It's fine.
HARI	You can see her in the morning.
NICK	Yeah.

Silence.

HARI	How've you been?
NICK	How've I been?
HARI	Have you been staying with friends or?
NICK	Friends.

33

HARI	We've not heard from you that's all
NICK	Sorry.
HARI	It's been three weeks so we were getting a bit
NICK	Were you?
HARI	Of course.
	Silence.
HARI	It's good to see you.
NICK	Yeah it's good to see you too.
	Pause.
HARI	You sure you don't want
NICK	I'd have a beer if you've got one.
HARI	A beer. Yeah sure why not? I'll join you. Why not have a beer?
NICK	We don't have to.
HARI	No a beer's alright isn't it?
	He gets two cans.
NICK	Thanks.
	Silence.
NICK	So
	Silence.
NICK	I've been having a
	Silence.
HARI	This is nice isn't it. Got it wholesale at Costco actually so it works out pretty good.
	Silence.
NICK	I was wondering if I could borrow a bit of money.
	Silence.

HARI	I thought we said
NICK	I know
HARI	Cos we did lend you for your pop-up café
NICK	I know but that wasn't my fault
HARI	And then when you needed to visit your girlfriend in Dublin after her opera
NICK	I know
HARI	And then for your TEFL course.
NICK	Yeah. It's fine.
	Pause.
HARI	It's not like we have loads of cash just swimming around.
NICK	I know.
HARI	So you'll be okay?
NICK	Of course.
	Silence.
NICK	I should push off.
HARI	What?
NICK	I should get going.
HARI	But you're not staying?
NICK	I can't.
HARI	You've not seen Mum.
NICK	Tell her I said hi.
HARI	Nick
NICK	I'm staying with a friend so
HARI	You're welcome to stay here.
NICK	Nah.

HARI	Stay here for a few days just shake yourself off a bit.
NICK	I'm fine.
HARI	We can spend some time together Mum would love to see
NICK	I can't.

Pause. HARI nods. NICK goes to the door.

HARI	Nick. Here take this at least okay. Just use it to get something to eat or.
NICK	Pret.
HARI	You will though yeah?
NICK	Of course.

Garage

They are polishing JÅN's parts. His head, separated from the rest of his body, rests on its own, but is animate.

MAX	We were thinking Jån that
JÅN	Yes?
HARI	Oh bloody hell.
MAX	Well wondering really
HARI	I've lost the belly button again.
MAX	Oh Hari.
JÅN	You were thinking what?

Beat. MAX and HARI look at each other. Big news.

MAX	That if you wanted you needn't stay
HARI	Only if you fancy a change
MAX	Yes only if you fancy
JÅN	Spit it out Max.

HARI	You needn't stay here in the garage.
MAX	We thought you could come into the house. Take the spare room.
HARI	It just feels a bit cold out here and well you're part of the family now aren't you?
MAX	It's only going spare anyway so
HARI	Ah here it is! *(Fishes it out of his pocket.)* Confused it with a 20p piece!
JÅN	I'd love that.
HARI	You would?
MAX	Then it's settled.

3

Basement

HARI	Now she's off!
JÅN	Look at her go!
HARI	Toot toot!
JÅN	I'd say we'll have the coal delivered before sundown at this rate.
HARI	Sundown? She'll be there by tea! Easy now, bring her down a bit, careful not to overheat the engine. That's it nice and steady. There. Now we just let her fly.
JÅN	Round and round.
BOTH	Toot toot!
	They watch it go.
JÅN	How long have you been into train sets?
HARI	God ages. Love the engineering side you know.
JÅN	Oh it's not a toy.
HARI	No quite.
JÅN	They're extraordinarily detailed aren't they all the models. Did you paint them yourself?
HARI	No they come painted.
JÅN	Still you fit them together really well.
HARI	Yes I do like the composition of the landscape. I fancy myself as a bit of a designer when it comes to this.
JÅN	I think I could really get into it myself.
	Silence. The train whizzes round.
JÅN	What's this piece?
HARI	Oh that's old, doesn't actually go with this set. Different sized tracks. Leave it there.

JÅN	There's loads here.
HARI	Yes I bought quite a lot of it at one point never quite took off. Don't worry about it.
JÅN	It's a bit bigger than this. Is it for kids or something?
HARI	Yes. Yes it's for kids.
JÅN	Barely been touched. This clock tower's not even been opened.
HARI	No. Hey come and have a look here, I'm about to change the signals.

JÅN returns. Silence as the train loops and loops.

HARI looks at JÅN. JÅN nods. HARI offers him the controller. JÅN takes it, but leaves his hands there holding HARI's.

HARI	You know
JÅN	Yes?
HARI	Here's a thought. Maybe you're just humouring me but
JÅN	What?
HARI	Well you might not be interested but. Never mind.
JÅN	Please.
HARI	I was going to say that if you like the look of that unused set feel free to help yourself.
JÅN	What?
HARI	You can have it if you like.
JÅN	I?
HARI	Be good to see it go to a good home.

Pause.

JÅN	I'm going to play with it every day.

Garden

MAX	Peonies.
JÅN	Peonies.
MAX	Roses.
JÅN	Roses.
MAX	Daffodils.
JÅN	Why do they call them daffodils?
MAX	I don't know. It's a nice name though isn't it?
JÅN	It's lovely.
MAX	These are foxgloves. They grow wild if you're not careful.
JÅN	I like learning about the flowers with you Max. It's nice.

Silence. They busy themselves arranging the flowers.

MAX	Jån.
JÅN	Yes?
MAX	You don't. You don't need to call me Max if you don't want. I mean you can but. I'd like. I'd like you to start calling me Mum. Would you do that?
JÅN	Alright then.
MAX	Thank you. That means a lot to me.

He smiles, and keeps working.

MAX	You have to prune the leaves to keep them all thriving.
JÅN	It's hard work.
MAX	It can be but the satisfaction is enormous. Just think when we're done we can enjoy the garden.
JÅN	Come out here and read.

MAX	Yes.
JÅN	Or have some friends over for a glass of wine.
MAX	Lovely idea.
JÅN	Or just come out here in the evening and take in the air.
MAX	My thoughts exactly.
JÅN	I could definitely get used to it. Oh stay still.
MAX	What is it?
JÅN	Here. A ladybird it was in your hair.
MAX	What a delicate little thing.
JÅN	It's beautiful.
MAX	Yes.

They watch it crawl on JÅN's finger.

MAX	Can I ask you something Jån?
JÅN	Of course.
MAX	What's it like in in in your I mean what's it like for you to.
JÅN	To?
MAX	I suppose I'm saying do you ever get things in your head and you just can't you can't shake them?
JÅN	Oh. Erm. I don't think so. To me the world just seems to fit. To fit into neat shapes.
MAX	Neat shapes.

JÅN smiles.

JÅN	Hey.
MAX	What, another?
JÅN	No it's
MAX	I'm sorry

JÅN	A little tear.
MAX	I think it's the pollen.
JÅN	It's okay.
MAX	The hayfever. I should probably go inside.
JÅN	No. Come on let's stay out here a bit longer. It's so nice, Mum.
	Pause.
MAX	Yes. Alright then.
	They watch the ladybird crawl along JÅN's finger.

Study

Night. Silence. On the desk is a camera, its little charging light glowing red.

The window slides open and NICK crawls through, looking worse than ever. He stands still for a second, taking in the room.

The door opens and HARI comes in. NICK has made for the window but stops.

HARI	What the – hey – what the
NICK	Shhhhh
HARI	Nick?!
NICK	Please shhhh
HARI	Nick what the hell are you
NICK	Please
HARI	Scared me half to death surprising me like that what were you thi
NICK	Shhh Dad please don't shout
HARI	How on earth did you get up here?
NICK	Please I just wanted to

HARI	I thought it was a burglar I thought I was gonna get burgled or raped or
NICK	Dad
HARI	Or
NICK	*Dad*
HARI	Christ.

Pause. HARI calms down.

HARI	God what is that? Oh Nick you – you stink.
NICK	Sorry.
HARI	Where have you been? You don't look you look terrible.
NICK	Alright.
HARI	You should have called first
NICK	I know

Silence.

HARI	What's that?
NICK	It's nothing. A scratch.
HARI	From a ruddy tiger you've been beaten up.
NICK	Don't worry about it.
HARI	But I do. That's the thing. I do.

Silence.

NICK	You look well.

Silence.

NICK	Nice bookshelves.
HARI	Thank you, they were doing a deal on them so.

Silence.

NICK	Is that new?

HARI	Huh?
	They look at the camera.
HARI	Yes. Mum got it for me.
	Silence.
HARI	No Nick.
NICK	No what?
HARI	You're going to rob your own house.
	Pause.
HARI	You're breaking into your own house to
NICK	Nobody's perfect Dad.
HARI	I'll call the police.
NICK	No.
HARI	I will I'll I'll call the police. And I'll wake Mum.
	Pause.
NICK	I'm sorry Dad.
	Silence.
HARI	You're going to die Nick.
NICK	Yeah. Well.
HARI	I wish you wouldn't. I wish you'd just I wish you'd just not left. I wish you'd just stayed in here with us and we'd kept on and you hadn't been
NICK	But I am.
HARI	I know.
NICK	That's how I am.
HARI	Yes but.
	NICK approaches the camera. They look at each other. He picks it up. HARI doesn't say anything. NICK goes to the window.

HARI	It's my birthday. You know that? It's my birthday today.
NICK	Yeah.
HARI	Is that why you came back?

Living Room

MAX	You have to Hari
JÅN	Give it a go
HARI	No I'm crap!
MAX	We're all crap that's why it's funny!
JÅN	Go on Hari we've all had a go
HARI	Alright alright bloody hell it's like being back at school here okay get ready with the timer
JÅN	Dun da da da
MAX	Ladies and gentlemen!
HARI	None of that come on let's just get on with it!
JÅN	Three. Two. One. Action.

HARI starts a mime. He's really crap. MAX and JÅN start cracking up.

MAX	Toad?

HARI shakes his head.

JÅN	Frog?

HARI shakes his head.

JÅN	Toad in the hole?

HARI shakes his head.

MAX	Toadstool.

HARI	It's nothing to do with bloody toads alright!
JÅN	Nananana!
MAX	Don't speak!

He continues. He really is terrible.

JÅN	What kind of thing is it?
HARI	It's a film.
MAX	Mime it don't say it!
JÅN	Have you ever played this game before?

Does the mime.

HARI	Film.

He keeps miming it.

MAX	How many words?
JÅN	Three words.
MAX	Whole thing.
JÅN	Angry.
MAX	Angry man.
JÅN	Fat man.
HARI	Steady on.

MAX and JÅN are really laughing now.

MAX	Killer!
JÅN	The Devil Wears Prada?
MAX	Where did that come from?
JÅN	Kill Bill?
MAX	Dead.
JÅN	Shoot. Shooting. Killing. Shoot.
MAX	Time.

| JAN | Good Will Hunting! |
| HARI | Yes! |

They all collapse in giggles.

TV Room

MAX and HARI are watching TV with JAN. HARI is half-heartedly reading the paper. The silence between them is easy, contented. After a while JAN begins idly doodling a tattoo on his forearm.

MAX looks around the room at her family, who continue with their little preoccupations.

HARI looks up and they catch each other's eyes.

They smile. Silence.

At length, HARI reaches for the remote and presses a button.

Kitchen

NICK is sitting at the table. He looks better than when we last saw him. He's getting better. In fact with his upright posture, his relaxed breathing, and the way he gently smiles at MAX as she potters about the kitchen we might almost think it's JAN.

NICK	I really like this kitchen.
MAX	You do?
NICK	Yeah. I forgot how much I liked it. I like the plants in the window and the toaster in the corner. I like the light coming through from the garden. I like I really like being back here.
MAX	Well we like having you back.
NICK	My flat's not like this I'm afraid.
MAX	No. No it's not like this.

NICK	It's not a nice home.
MAX	No.
NICK	This is a nice home. No one would prefer that home to this one would they?
MAX	Well you can stay as long as you like.

Pause.

MAX	I tell you what. Why don't you sit there and I'll toast you a bagel.
NICK	Okay.

She starts working in silence.

NICK	How have you kept this!
MAX	What? Oh I like it!
NICK	Mum I did this when I was like five.
MAX	It's sweet!
NICK	Why have I done the house in purple?
MAX	I think you'd run out of red.
NICK	Come to that why is Dad green!?
MAX	Haha – I like the way the sun is sort of staring at us like –
NICK	Ha! He looks like some sort of sex pest!

They laugh at the drawing. Pause.

NICK	I'm gonna do it this time Mum.

She looks at him.

NICK	I can feel it. This is the one. I want you to know that. It's not that I don't want to be better, I do. I do. I do. That's all I want. I know I've let you down and that I'm probably the worst son in the world. I don't want to be, I really don't. I want to stay here to stay here

and be clean and live with you guys. I really really
really really really really want that.

She nods.

MAX   Good. Because you know Nicky, there is nothing
nothing I would like more than that.

Silence.

MAX   Now how about that bagel?

Kitchen

HARI, MAX, LAURIE, PAUL, AMY and NICK sit at the table having brunch.

LAURIE   Mm these are delicious Hari, wow aren't these good
Ames?

AMY   Fantastic.

HARI   Oh well Nick helped as it happens.

NICK   I cracked the eggs.

Everyone laughs.

MAX   No no but he did more than that, you did more than
that Nick, don't do yourself down.

HARI   Yes Nick was, what do they call it on Masterchef,
Nick was my Sous Chef!

PAUL   Very good.

MAX   So how's school Amy?

AMY   Not bad thanks.

HARI   Your A-levels must be coming up.

AMY   Yeah we just had our mocks.

LAURIE   Amy was pulling her hair out with stress. Honestly
in our day we were allowed to mess up, play around,
have a second chance. For her, you know because

she's got that offer from Oxford, she really has
no margin for error so it's just pressure pressure
pressure.

AMY   Thanks Mum.

LAURIE   No but you know what I mean.

HARI   Well congratulations on your offer Amy, that's, that's
               really something to be very proud of well done. Even
               if you don't get the grades now you know at least
               you've had the offer.

NICK   Dad.

HARI   What no I don't mean it like that I mean.

MAX   Oh Hari.

HARI   She knows what I mean. I'm sure you'll get the grades
               I'm just saying. Ignore me.

AMY   Haha it's okay Hari, I know what you meant. To be
               honest I'm really not that stressed about it. I think I
               might even prefer to go to Bristol anyway.

PAUL   A lot of her friends are going to Bristol so.

LAURIE   How are you Nick, how's the café?

PAUL   Hari told us you were trying to start up a little café?

NICK   Oh, yeah, well it was more of a sort of food van
               thing to be honest like for festivals and stuff.

PAUL   Ah okay, and?

NICK   It was good but getting into all the good festivals was
               really hard cos I think they've been working with all
               the same people for years and don't want anyone new
               so.

               Silence.

LAURIE   Well it's great that you gave it a go.

PAUL	I think it's a good thing. Bill Gates dropped out of uni didn't he? Country needs more entrepreneurs. The best idea is the next idea know what I mean?

Pause.

LAURIE Or if you've got a passion for cooking you could try getting some experience in a restaurant first. You know build up your knowledge base then branch out on your own.

NICK To be honest it was more of a way to get into festivals but yeah that is a good idea.

Pause.

PAUL So it's music you're into then? Well you're still young, you should start your own band. Hey what was that band Hari that started in your school?

HARI Coldplay.

PAUL That's it, see everyone's got to start somewhere.

AMY Coldplay started at Bart's?

HARI Well one of them went there. The drummer I think.

LAURIE Start a band now, practise hard, you could be playing those festivals in few years.

NICK I don't know. I'm not that good at music to be honest. Just like listening to it I guess.

Silence.

MAX Nick's doing really well. We're really proud of him, aren't we Hari?

HARI Yeah. Dead proud.

NICK Thanks guys.

MAX He's been through a lot but he's on the home straight.

LAURIE Of course he is.

PAUL   To Nick! *(They all toast.)* Listen, Nick. This might not be of any interest to you but, if you like, when you feel ready, you're very welcome to come and have a few shifts at the shop?

NICK   Really?

HARI   Seriously Paul? That's very kind.

PAUL   He'd be doing me a favour – we're always looking for good new people.

LAURIE   Only to tide you over, you know, until you want to go back to college maybe, or apply for a course or

PAUL   Oh it's not a job for life – just a bit of pocket money.

MAX   What do you say Nick?

            NICK is truly touched. He nods, choked up.

NICK   I'd. I'd really like. Thanks Paul.

HARI   You better watch out though, he'll be running the bloody company in a few years and might fire your lazy arse!

PAUL   Haha, fine by me I could do with a bit more time with my good friend Mr. Nine Iron.

LAURIE   It's so lovely what you've done with this room, Hari, I think it every time I come round.

HARI   So much lighter isn't it? I did all the joining myself as it happens. Why pay someone good money for something you can teach yourself on YouTube?

            As the others talk, MAX and NICK share a warm smile. She reaches and squeezes him affectionately on the arm. He smiles.

Teenage Boy's Bedroom

Evening. NICK is sitting alone.

He gets up and picks his phone off the desk. He returns to the bed and swipes through some things, then puts it down.

He opens his laptop, and idly checks some things, glancing at his phone as well but, bored, gives up on that too. He closes the computer. He drops the phone on the bed.

He goes to the window and looks out.

He steps away from the window and takes a deep breath.

He goes back to the window and opens it. The sounds from the suburban street outside drift in. He leans out of the window and breathes it in. He comes back into the room and steps away from the window again.

He freezes. He shakes his head. He knows.

He takes a backpack from under the bed and puts his laptop in it. He puts his phone in his pocket.

He goes back to the window and climbs out, feet first, until only his torso is visible, preparing to shimmy down the drainpipe.

The door opens, and MAX comes in carefully holding a mug of hot chocolate.

MAX   I thought you might like

        She sees NICK, his body half out the window. They look at each other. Pause.

NICK   I'm just going to meet Amy. She said some of her friends were getting together so.

        Pause.

NICK   I'll be back in an hour.

        They look at each other.

MAX   Please. Nick please.

        A pause. And then, he goes.

        MAX stands in the empty room, looking at the empty window.

Conservatory

MAX stands in the empty room, looking at the window.

MAX   Hari!

                 HARI enters.

MAX   I've changed my mind. I think we should have Laurie
                 and Paul round to meet Jån.

HARI   I thought you said

MAX   I said I've changed my mind Hari is it *that* fucking
                 hard to understand?

                 Beat.

HARI   I'll send them an email.

4

Attic

HARI is staring at JÅN, glass-eyed. MAX has fallen asleep against the wall.

JÅN   Nothing gives me more pleasure than a good book don't you agree? The themes, the characters, the feeling of wholesomeness one gets from simply getting lost in good words and what *(Beep.)* I was thinking tomorrow we could maybe go into town and see if we can find that Diesel Shunter you were talking abou *(Beep.)* Okay, okay I'll go first. Um, alright, got one: Vegetab *(Beep.)* And if I just shift this finger then that's offsp *(Beep.)* There *(Beep.)* How *(Beep.)* Some *(Beep.)* You're the best.

     Pause.

JÅN   I really mean that. The best Dad in the world.

     HARI looks at MAX, checking she's asleep. Beep.

JÅN   This may sound a bit disloyal but

HARI   It's alright. What's on your mind?

JÅN   I just feel like, having thought about everything that happened, you know with Nick that.

HARI   What?

JÅN   Well if Max had just listened to you, you know, if she'd been a little more patient.

HARI   A little more trusting I suppose you could say.

JÅN   Then maybe I don't know maybe things would have turned out differently.

HARI   My point of view was simply that nothing is beyond repair. Take the stuff up here for example. This fax machine. A lot of people might give up the ghost. Might think of it as junk. But my point of view is – always has been – that with a bit of perseverance you can always find a use for anything.

JÅN	Nothing should be just… thrown away.
HARI	I tried to explain that to her. I tried but she wouldn't listen. She insisted Jån she said if he ever came back we had to turn him away. Do you believe that? Turn him awa
	MAX stirs. HARI notices, quietening down. Then, after he's sure MAX has settled again – beep.
JÅN	If she'd only listened to you.

Airing Cupboard

MAX and JÅN iron and fold. MAX hasn't slept in days.

JÅN	Do I have to perform?
MAX	Of course not, you just need to
JÅN	To?
MAX	Be the engaged, polite personality you always are. I just want them to meet you, simple as that.
JÅN	I can see why you like ironing. Getting everything flat and fresh and folded away.
MAX	Hari even likes his underwear done, can you imagine?
	They smile.
JÅN	Doesn't Laurie go on and on about Amy. I mean Jesus it gets to the point where you're like alright already I get it we all love Amy but enough.
MAX	It's not her fault. She doesn't know what it's like to to have to deal with.
JÅN	I'm just saying it's all been so easy for her.
MAX	She's had an easy ride of it that's what Hari says.
JÅN	If she had been through what you and Hari had

MAX	Well
JÅN	God you'd see that facade crack soon enough don't you think?
MAX	I don't know. I wouldn't wish it on
JÅN	Imagine her trying to cope with what the two of you
MAX	Yes. Maybe.
JÅN	And what makes it worse is that silent judgement.

MAX reaches for the remote control. Beep. Pause.

JÅN	What makes it worse is that smug little bitchy judgement face.
MAX	You mustn't say things like that Jån.
JÅN	If I were you sometimes I'd wish Nick had got Amy involved too then she'd see.

Beep.

JÅN	Sometimes I'd wish it had been Amy not Nick.

Beep.

JÅN	Sometimes I'd wish Nick had gone out with Amy and that he'd fucked her stupid perfect little brains out.

Beeep. He holds up a pair of beautifully ironed y-fronts.

JÅN	How's that?
MAX	Perfect.

Attic

NICK	I've got some news. I know I've been away for a bit and you were probably worried and I can totally understand why. I'm sorry I haven't been in touch but I didn't want to get your hopes up and then let you down again because I know I've done that too many

times already. I've been getting myself straightened out. It's been hard work it's been really hard work but I did it. I'm better now. I don't expect you to trust me or even to like me much at first, but I came here today to promise you that even if it takes the rest of my life I'm going to show you that I'm better.

HARI looks at MAX, she's welling up. She nods.

HARI   You don't need to apologise darling. We forgive you. Do you want to come and stay here for a bit? I could get the Dyson out and have your room spick and span in no time.

NICK   Thanks but, I've actually got my own place.

MAX   Your own place.

NICK   Yeah. Like I said I didn't want to get your hopes up so I didn't tell you but, once I felt better I started looking for work. I ended up taking Paul up on his offer. I begged him not to say anything because I didn't want to let you down if I couldn't handle it. I really enjoyed it, keeping inventories, managing stock. After a while Paul and Laurie were so impressed they asked me to take over from Monique when she left to have a baby.

HARI   Isn't she the store manager?

NICK smiles.

NICK   Saved up enough money to rent a little one bed near the station. You'd be proud dad, I put all the furniture together myself even put up a few bookshelves too.

HARI   Furniture.

MAX   Bookshelves.

NICK   I've had Paul and Laurie round – they said it was even nicer than Amy's flat.

HARI   I don't know what to say.

NICK	Say you'll come round for dinner maybe? My treat?
MAX	Of course. Of course we will.
NICK	I thought you might tell me to go away and never come back. I thought after last time you might not want anything to do with me.
MAX	Never.
HARI	Never.
NICK	I thought you might have said to each other

Pause.

HARI	What?
MAX	What did you think we'd have said?
NICK	I thought you might have said enough is enough. I thought you might have said you've been through so much that you couldn't do it again.
HARI	No
NICK	I thought you might have said that if I ever came back you'd tell me that you were cutting me out of your lives for good.
MAX	We wouldn't do that. We would never give up on you Nick.
HARI	No.
NICK	I'd understand Mum. I'd understand if you had done.

Pause.

MAX	So what are you making us for this dinner?
NICK	How does lamb sound?
MAX	Yum.
HARI	What with?
NICK	Potatoes
HARI	Ooh

NICK	And greens
HARI	Delish
NICK	And swimming.

Beat.

HARI	And what?
JÅN	And swimming.
MAX	Swimming?
JÅN	Swimming swimming swimming swimming swimming swimmi

Beep. JÅN pauses, alive but unspeaking. Silence.

| MAX | I had a dream last night. I was here, in the house, but the layout of the rooms was different. There were new corridors and landings where I had no idea we had even applied for planning permission. They house seemed to go on and on, doors and landings and towers and stairways I couldn't find the end of it. In some rooms were things I recognised, the fireplace, the ultrasonic humidifier, but others opened up to new rooms wonderful and strange. I opened a door and saw the ocean stretched out in front of me. I climbed into the attic and a whole forest had grown. Inside the airing cupboard was packed the whole universe. I stood at the door and watched it float. As I made my way downstairs I realised that the ground floor must be medieval; the floors were red brick. Everywhere it was gloomy and dark. I came upon a heavy door and when I opened it I discovered a stone stairway, leading down into the depths. I descended as far as it would go, past cellars and caverns I had never seen before. These must be the foundations of the house I thought. How funny that I've never been down here. At the very bottom of the stairs was a cave cut into the rock. To think that this was beneath our feet the whole time we've |

lived here. Thick dust lay on the floor and in the dust were scattered stones and broken shards of pottery, as if discarded by some primitive culture. As I lent in, getting to my hands and knees to examine more closely, I realised that these weren't bits of pottery at all. They were bones. I picked up a skull from the pile but, just as I began to turn it around to face me, I woke up.

HARI   I dreamt I was batting at number five for Middlesex.

Beep.

JÅN   I thought you might tell me to go away and never come back. I thought after last time you might not want anything to do with me me me me me me.

Beep. JÅN pauses.

MAX   How did it go with the engineer?

HARI   He said these things are cheap as chips. They go wrong all the time and the truth is no one knows why. Give him another chance and if it keeps happening then

MAX   What?

HARI   Get rid.

Dining Room

Night. MAX and NICK are talking. NICK looks worse than we've ever seen him.

NICK   Where's Dad?

MAX   Your father's upstairs.

NICK   I'd like to see him.

MAX   No.

NICK   No?

MAX	That's not a good idea.
NICK	I'm sorry I upset you. I just needed to get it out of my system but now I can focus on getting better. If I can put the deposit down on this flat I I need to explain it to Dad.
MAX	That's not going to happen.
NICK	He'll understand. I need to talk to him.
MAX	Nick. You're talking to me.
	Silence.
NICK	I made a mistake
MAX	No
NICK	I know I fucked up but can't we
MAX	Nick
NICK	I'm just asking for help
MAX	Please
NICK	Just a bit of help. I needed to fuck up to know what I need to do now
MAX	We're not going to help you this time.
NICK	Let me
MAX	We're not going to lend you any money or help you out with this flat. We're not going to let you stay here again.
NICK	I'm not asking
MAX	We're not paying for another rehab, we're not borrowing more money just so you can
NICK	I'll pay it ba
MAX	We've tried and tried but now you're on you're
NICK	I want to speak to Dad.
MAX	You're speaking to Mum! Okay? You're speaking to Mum. And she's telling you – it's over.

Silence.

MAX	If you check yourself in somewhere then maybe
NICK	You want me to be perfect
MAX	We'll try to be involved
NICK	You want me to be pristine and clean and have no scratches
MAX	If you've made that decision yourself
NICK	But that's not what people are like
MAX	Not financially but we could visit
NICK	I don't want fixing. I don't need it.
MAX	Yes you do.
NICK	I like how I am.
MAX	No you don't. You're dirty and you stink and your eyes are sunken into your head.
NICK	You don't know anything.
MAX	You're unwell.
NICK	So?
MAX	You're miserable.
NICK	No.
MAX	You're wretched.
NICK	That's what you need to think. You need to think I'm ill because you can't understand that I might have chosen this. You're scared because I might have chosen something different to you and Dad. You're scared because you're starting to realise that maybe I actually know what's going on. Maybe I've walked through this house, seen the TV room, seen the nice garden, seen the clean fridge and thought, you know what, I'd rather be high.
MAX	No.

65

NICK	That I would willingly sacrifice all this to be high.
MAX	No.
NICK	You think I don't know what I'm doing. But if I could go back to the very first time and I could see exactly what it would do to me, where I'd end up, how much I'd lose, I'd take it in a second. Every single time.

Silence.

MAX	We're not going to help you this time Nick.
NICK	I want to speak to Dad.
MAX	No. This is the end.

5

Dining Room

MAX, HARI, JÅN, LAURIE, PAUL and AMY are having dinner. They eat in comfortable silence.

JÅN wipes his mouth with a napkin neatly. LAURIE and PAUL glance at JÅN, impressed. HARI and MAX share a smile, proud.

JÅN	This is delicious Dad thank you so much.
HARI	Yes it's come out quite well in the end I have to say.
	LAURIE and PAUL look at MAX like 'what a polite boy!'
JÅN	Can I pour anyone some water?
AMY	Thank you.
PAUL	I could get used to this kind of service!
JÅN	It's no trouble.
	He pours the water, and they smile, impressed.
HARI	So you're down for the weekend are you Amy?
AMY	Yeah. Going back tomorrow.
MAX	And how's it going up there?
AMY	Yeah okay thanks.
LAURIE	She's loving it.
AMY	It's hard work but yeah it's what I want to do I guess so
LAURIE	She's in the Freshers play.
AMY	Mum.
MAX	Is she indeed?
LAURIE	I warned her you'll be worn out but what did you say to me Amy?
AMY	It doesn't matter.
LAURIE	She said 'that's what Pro Plus is for'!

AMY	It was a joke.
PAUL	In our day we took drugs to *avoid* work – isn't that right Hari?
MAX	Very admirable.
LAURIE	She's burning the candle at both ends you see because she's got her heart set on neurology.
AMY	Mum that's literally years
MAX	Neurology!
LAURIE	I'd always fancied neurology myself but never quite had the guts to go for it so I'm just thrilled that Amy has.
HARI	Must be terribly competitive.
PAUL	One in a hundred roughly.
LAURIE	And that's only including medical students of course.
HARI	Yes of course.
LAURIE	So think of all the ones who didn't even get into medical school.
AMY	Oh my god.
PAUL	You're looking at extremely long odds.
JÅN	Well very best of luck.
HARI	I remember you sitting at this table going at your pasta with a knife *reee reee reee* I didn't think then I'd fancy have you open my head up!
MAX	Hari.
LAURIE	And she's got a bloke as well.
AMY	Mum why?
LAURIE	Adam. But everyone calls him Coops.
PAUL	His name's Cooper.
AMY	And his phone number's 079

LAURIE	They asked!
AMY	Can we change the subject?
LAURIE	How about you Jån, how do you spend your days?
PAUL	Apart from helping out these old codgers!
JÅN	I'm looking for a course at the moment actually. Trying to go to University.
AMY	University? Right, is that-?
LAURIE	Do you have an idea what you'd like to study?
JÅN	I'm doing pretty well at most subjects but I think my real passion lies in management and hospitality.
PAUL	Nice. Lots of good jobs out there in that kind of field.
HARI	Exactly what I told him.
JÅN	When Dad applied to Uni he didn't really know what to do so just kind of fell into education. I don't want to make that mistake.
LAURIE	Is that true Hari?
HARI	In a manner of speaking yes. I always thought I'd be really good at running a restaurant, you know I have a passion for food.
AMY	The lamb is really lovely by the way.
HARI	Fancied myself starting a sort of café, then maybe building it up into a little franchise you know.
PAUL	Sounds a bit more interesting than making sure year 10 have their shirts tucked in.
HARI	Still, no regrets.
PAUL	No quite.
HARI	But I'm glad that Jån wants to follow that passion.
LAURIE	Nice to see him take after you.

JÅN	I'd also like to do a design subsid. Or maybe do an evening course in design.
LAURIE	Ooh taking after Max now.
MAX	Stop it I'll blush.
JÅN	I think the design of a space is so important. Even room by room, it frames the way we interact with the world. The right choice of chair or curve of a frame can genuinely alter our mood. It's a reflection of who we are.
MAX	I couldn't agree more.
LAURIE	Fascinating.

LAURIE gives MAX a raised eyebrow, impressed.

HARI	And actually Jån's got a little girlfriend too, haven't you Jån?
JÅN	It's not serious.
PAUL	Take my advice, Jån, you never know it's serious until it's too late!
JÅN	Well we've just started seeing each other really.
PAUL	How did you meet?
JÅN	She's a prostitute working out of Reading.
PAUL	Excuse me?
MAX	You didn't tell us that Jån.
JÅN	Oh, didn't I? Yes we met on one of my visits to that brothel.
HARI	Er Jån I'm not sure
JÅN	I'd been a few times before but I'd not really fallen for any of the other girls particularly. But then when I met Danika and we got talking I just thought yes I could really go for this girl.

PAUL	Well I suppose that's sort of sweet in a way. What was it you liked about her?
MAX	I don't think we need to
JÅN	Well she looks really young for a start, like sort of fifteen or so. And she said she'd be happy to do anal if I paid her extra. I like anal because it's a tighter hole but some of the girls are a bit reluctant
HARI	Alright mate I think that's enough.
JÅN	Oh.
MAX	It's not really dinner table talk okay darling.
JÅN	Sorry. I just wanted to tell you about this girl.
MAX	Why don't you talk about your restaurant instead, that sounds interesting?
JÅN	Okay. Well like Dad said I'd like to start small and hopefully one day expand it. I want to do sort of really low quality fried chicken and chips, that sort of place. I've had a look at the numbers and if you buy scrap meat from the right abattoir you can save unbelievable costs, then once they're packed together in a nugget or a pie or something no one really knows the difference anyway. I think the margins are really attractive and, if I can find a location near a secondary school, I think I can really get a lot of passing trade as schools now have to serve very healthy lunches at low cost so they taste terrible and everyone goes out anyway. My dream is to one day own a fried chicken place in front of every school in England!

Beat.

LAURIE	But, aren't you worried that it might not be good for the kids?
JÅN	Sorry?

LAURIE	That, you know, they might eat too much of this stuff?
JÅN	I want them to eat too much of it. Didn't you hear the business plan? That's the whole idea.
HARI	Shall we change the subject?
JÅN	I was just trying to think of a way to make a good living. Should I not have
LAURIE	Have you guys watched the Wire?
MAX	Oh! Have we!
PAUL	Seasons three and four – mwah.
AMY	I thought season two was a bit less
HARI	But, as a body of work
LAURIE	Novelistic, actually. In my opinion it's novelistic.
JÅN	I actually think the Wire's overrated. Isn't it just quite boring?

They all look at him.

AMY	These carrots are delicious Hari.
HARI	Thank you, I
JÅN	I've changed my mind. I'm sorry about before, I was being stupid. About the chicken and Danika and stuff. I don't really love Danika, I was only joking. And of course the Wire is brilliant. It's the closest thing this century has to Dickensian social observation.
HARI	Okay, that's better.
MAX	He does this you see, he's always trying to self-improve.
JÅN	And the chicken was a stupid idea. I think I'd rather sell organic tacos with a vegan twist.
LAURIE	That sounds lovely.

JÅN	Or Moroccan influenced burritos.
PAUL	Mmmm.
JÅN	Or locally sourced chutneys. I haven't decided yet. But I know I want it to be good. I want it to be successful. But I don't just mean financially; the most important thing is the quality of the work
PAUL	Wow, he's got his head screwed on – no pun intended Hari.
JÅN	But in fact the quality of the work is just a route not a destination. The destination is the pride I will take from the work itself. And the pride I'll take from the pride you'll take in me.
LAURIE	Gosh.
AMY	Is he
JÅN	There is a pride in work and a pride in produce. I know that certain products are better than others. An apple is better than a cigarette. A toaster is better than a bong. A netball is better than a beer can. I want to surround myself with good things. I want to take pride in my surroundings. I want to learn and be better and I think I am, I'm trying anyway
HARI	*(Starting to sense a growing mania.)* Would anyone like a coffee? Jån shall we
JÅN	Because that is the most important thing: happiness. Mental wellbeing. I know that I want to grow old and wise one day. I want to be full of pride and satisfaction and happiness. But not the wrong kind of happiness.
HARI	Jån.
JÅN	Not artificial happiness, but organic happiness. I know from Mum and Dad that that's all they want.
LAURIE	That's… sweet.
HARI	Let's change the subject shall we?

74

LAURIE	Amy why don't you tell them about the film society you
JÅN	I'd like to be a human rights lawyer one day.
HARI	Okay Jån.
JAN	I'd like to take a year out to work for an NGO.
MAX	Jan.
JÅN	I'd like to write novels that subtly reflect the contemporary condition.
AMY	Maybe we should
JÅN	I'd like to marry Amy!
HARI	*(Trying to cover.)* Ah, that's a sweet thought Jån.
JÅN	Yes yes yes I'd like the two of us to have the kind of happiness that she and Coops have now.
AMY	Mum?
JÅN	That's what I want. I want to be the kind of guy that Amy likes. The kind of guy that Paul and Laurie likes.
LAURIE	We do –
	JÅN grabs AMY by the arm.
AMY	Ah!
JÅN	I want me and Amy to get married and move back here to live really nearby
AMY	Get off Jån.
MAX	Jån let her go.
JÅN	*(Dragging her to her feet.)* I want us to have children and be a happy family just like all of you guys.
AMY	Ah – Hari tell him to
PAUL	Jån get off, do you understand, get off her.
JÅN	I want us to have beautiful perfect children that we will love

THOMAS ECCLESHARE

He pushes her down onto the table, standing over her, wrestling with her arms. The adults scream and stand, shocked. JÅN begins to pull at her skirt, fumble with his fly as PAUL and HARI jump in.

AMY   What the fuck are you

PAUL   Hey!

AMY   Ah!

HARI   Jån!

HARI and PAUL wrestle JÅN from AMY, calming him down. AMY scrabbles up from the table towards the door, away from them all.

MAX   Amy I I'm sorry I

AMY looks at MAX. Pause. AMY collects her bag from her chair and goes to the door. She turns to face MAX again.

AMY   I'm really sorry about Nick, Max. I miss him. I didn't know him well but I looked up to him a lot and I really I really liked him. He was the guy who was older than me I don't know if that means anything to you but it meant a lot to me. He was always the year ahead, always a few steps ahead and now and soon and this year I'll overtake him and that's made me really sad. I wanted to come here today to tell you that to tell you how great I thought Nick was. Thank you for a lovely dinner.

AMY goes.

LAURIE   Come on Paul.

JÅN   I'm sorry. I was trying trying to be good.

MAX   No, don't go. You don't have to go.

JÅN   Sorry sorry sorry

MAX   We can laugh about this. This is stupid really. Hari, say something.

HARI	Would anyone like a fruit tea?
LAURIE	Paul, now.
	They begin to gather their things.
MAX	Laurie please. Don't go.
JÅN	I'm trying to be polite Mum. I I'm – Laurie you look really nice this evening.
LAURIE	Paul!
JÅN	That shirt is a lovely colour on you.
MAX	He can be good, I promise. Jån say something nice.
JÅN	I fantasise about your lips on my cock.
HARI	Jesus Christ
PAUL	Right that's it.
JÅN	I'm sorry Paul, is that offensive?
LAURIE	Thanks Hari, thanks Max.
JÅN	It's okay Paul, I fantasise about your lips on my cock too.
MAX	Jån!
HARI	Guys wait, he doesn't mean it, you don't need to rush off.
PAUL	We said we'd Skype with Cal when we got back. He's on a training camp in Australia so the time difference, you know.
JÅN	I'm sorry I'm sorry I'm sorry I ruined it. Don't go please don't go I can do better I promise I can do better.
LAURIE	Goodbye Hari.
JÅN	I want to be the CEO of a huge company.
PAUL	Bye Max.
JÅN	I want to be the editor of a national newspaper.

MAX	Please

PAUL and LAURIE go. HARI follows after them.

JÅN	I want to have a job I want to have a conversation I want to have a bath I just want to be able to have a bath tomorrow I want to
MAX	Jån!
HARI	*(Off.)* Paul! Laurie! Come on, there's no need to go.
JÅN	I'm so sorry.
MAX	Don't.
JÅN	Mum?
MAX	Oh Jån.
JÅN	Mum Mum Mum Mum Mum Mum
MAX	No Jån.
JÅN	Mum Mum Mum Mum
MAX	Jån?

Front Garden

HARI	Paul wait!
PAUL	Sorry mate, it's just, Cal's waiting you know and it's all got a bit
LAURIE	*(Off.)* Paul!
PAUL	Yeah, coming love.
HARI	It's only a blip. Honestly give me five minutes with a screwdriver, I'm telling you he'll be right as rain. Please mate just come back inside. For Max. She was really excited about tonight. She just wanted to show we just wanted
LAURIE	*(Off.)* Paul!

HARI	We just wanted you to be impressed with him.
PAUL	Hari, I don't know how to say this but, the boy's a machine okay. Even before he had his little meltdown it's a bit. I mean all that looking to the future stuff, university, getting a job, isn't it a bit, it's a bit weird.
HARI	Wh-? What do you mean?
PAUL	We went along with it when it was a bit of fun when it was inside the house but this is is
HARI	What?
PAUL	It's like you're you're actually raising him or something. Like a, I mean, why bother? What's it all for?
HARI	For... love.

The sound of a car engine starts.

PAUL	I'll see you soon alright Hari.

PAUL goes. The sound of a car leaving. HARI watches it disappear down the street. Then, a huge banging noise comes from the house.

Destroyed Hallway

MAX	Hari, Hari!
HARI	Right where is he?
MAX	Something's malfunctioned I couldn't turn him off
HARI	Where is he?
MAX	I tried fiddling with the remote but the damned thing has so many functions
HARI	Max
MAX	You're never in the right mode

HARI	Max
MAX	And then if you are in the mode you've not got them on the right setting
HARI	Max!
MAX	I couldn't control him. I'm sorry.
HARI	I've only walked them to their car what on earth's happened?
MAX	He was shaken he was out of control stuck in some sort of malfunction I I I couldn't – he ran into the living room
HARI	Keep calm.
MAX	I followed. I tried to soothe him
HARI	And
MAX	And he's st st staring at the wall like I said moaning. I should have I don't know I didn't know what to do Hari I didn't know what to do
HARI	Did he hurt you?
MAX	He was just moaning I was trying to speak to him but I couldn't I couldn't
HARI	It's okay
MAX	He wouldn't listen nothing was getting through. I reached for the remote but before I could do anything he just switches. I was scared.

Destroyed Sitting Room

MAX	He picked up the television. Smashed it against the wall and the cables all ripped out of the sockets. Glass flew everywhere. I had to duck behind the sofa for cover. I scrambled for the remote but it had got

	mixed up with all the DVD ones and the Sonos thing and
HARI	It's got a little red label that's why I made the labels.
MAX	I couldn't read the labels could I because Jån was smashing the room to smithereens by using the lamp as a makeshift baseball bat! I was fumbling trying to find the right one, trying to calm him down but it was no good. I followed him back to the kitchen.

Destroyed Kitchen

MAX	But he had already got to the fridge pulling everything out emptying the veg tray.
HARI	Oh Max.
MAX	He was screaming and shouting.
HARI	What on earth about?
MAX	About nonsense about nothing about nonsense stuff. He's got this look in his eyes like he's just gone like his wiring's just gone and there I am banging away at those stupid buttons as he smashes through the conservatory,

Destroyed Conservatory

MAX	Rampaging through my pots and ripping up the flowers, back inside, into the hall

Destroyed Hall

MAX	Pulling the photos off the wall and smashing them against the paint.

HARI   This is supposed to be a premium product

MAX   I'd almost given up on the remote I was trying to reason with him

HARI   Never in my life

MAX   Find out what was on his mind. But he was already upstairs.

Destroyed Bed

MAX   Crashing into things

Destroyed Bathroom

MAX   Tearing rooms apart

Destroyed Study

MAX   It was like a madman in the house it was like

HARI   Don't Max

MAX   It was like

HARI   My printer!

Destroyed Landing

MAX   Eventually he ended up here. Closed the door and hasn't come out since.

    Silence.

HARI   Do you still have the remote?

She hands it over.

HARI   You see here's the label it's very clear.

Death stare.

HARI   But yes of course you were under pressure so fair
        enough. Right.

He knocks. No answer.

HARI   Jån? You're not in any trouble. We just want to talk.

Silence.

HARI   Jån mate, we're going to come in alright?

Teenage Boy's Room

JÅN has let them in. It's a teenage boy's room, as messy as the day it was left. Silence.

HARI   Haven't been up here for a while.

MAX   No.

HARI   We keep meaning to get it cleaned up don't we?

MAX   Yes.

HARI   Should get a zipvan or something, just blitz it one
        weekend. I could ask Tone if he fancies giving us a
        hand actually.

JÅN   I could give you a hand.

HARI   What were we talking about a few months ago Max, a
        study for you?

MAX   A gym.

HARI   That's right a gym.

She nods. Silence.

HARI   So.

MAX nods.

JÅN   I'm sorry I hurt Amy. I'm sorry I ruined the dinner
               party. I didn't mean to I don't know what. I don't
               know why I. It won't happen again.

               HARI gestures to give him his hand. JÅN holds out his hand.
               HARI takes it.

HARI   I'm sorry Jån.

               He begins to unscrew his left hand.

JÅN   It won't. I promise it won't.

               HARI continues to screw.

JÅN   Please.

MAX   Give me your hand love.

JÅN   Mum.

MAX   Here, give me your hand.

               MAX takes his other hand in hers.

JÅN   Dad.

MAX   That's it.

JÅN   Please don't do this.

HARI   It's okay.

JÅN   I don't know what happened. I'll try again let's try
               again.

HARI   I'm sorry Jan.

JÅN   I promise.

               The hands come off. They begin to untwist the elbows.

JÅN   Dad don't please please I promise. I can do better
               I will I'll do better. I must have short circuited or
               something some kind of processing problem or a
               software malfunction. Don't do this Mum. Please
               don't give up on me. Please don't

MAX   It's okay love.

And now the shoulders.

JÅN   Please

JÅN's arm comes loose with a gaggle of wires hanging loose at the join.

HARI   Jån listen to me. You've been fantastic for us, and we've loved having you. But Max and I saw something, a particular something, with certain specifications and certain guarantees of quality and unfortunately – it's not your fault – but it's just not been quite what we were expecting.

HARI reaches for the back of JÅN's head.

JÅN   Was I broken from the start do you think?

They look at him.

HARI   I don't know love. I'm sorry.

They turn him off and he crumples to the floor. MAX and HARI stand in silence, surrounded by the carnage of their child, parts of his body scattered around the room.

MAX holds up JÅN's separated hand and stares at it.

MAX   I'm sorry.

HARI   It's not your fault, the remote was

MAX   Not him. Not him.

Silence.

MAX   That night when he came to me.

HARI   I should have joined you.

MAX   And I turned him away.

HARI   I should have supported you.

MAX   How could a mother do that?

HARI   We both decided. I mean that Max we both

MAX   How could a mother give up?

HARI	We thought it was the only way.
MAX	That was the last time he was here. It was only a couple of weeks before he. And when he was at the door. When I was showing him out that night and I saw he had a cut on his finger.

MAX looks at the hand she's holding.

MAX	It wasn't even a bad one, and God knows he'd had some scratches on him over the years. He held it up to me and it was like he was just a kid again. A little kid with a scratch. And I took his finger in my hand, an adult's hand, a man's hand now, all dirty and grimy and and and I kissed it better. And you know what? I thought it would work. I thought in that moment, as I said goodbye, I thought that little kiss would make that finger better, just like when he was five.
HARI	Maybe it did? Maybe that finger got better. But there are so many parts. So many parts deep inside that we couldn't get to.
MAX	Yes.

She drops the hand. Silence.

MAX	I don't know if I can face it Hari. I don't know if I can.
HARI	I know.
MAX	I just want to feel better.
HARI	I know. I know.

Silence. He holds her. He looks at what's left of JAN and loosens his grip. She regains her composure and notices JAN too. They stare at him. And as they stare, a thought begins to crystallise in their minds. A thought as clean and pristine as a flatpacked wardrobe.

MAX	Neat shapes.

Silence.

HARI	It wouldn't be that hard. The truth is most of this is just casing. In theory there's no reason you couldn't
MAX	Uh huh.
HARI	Slide it in and hook it up
MAX	Because I'm finding mine so messy.
HARI	Me too.
MAX	It's tiring me out.
HARI	I wake up in the night do you?
MAX	Yes.
HARI	I wake up and I've just got so many
MAX	Yes
HARI	Thoughts.
MAX	Me too.
HARI	It's tiring.
MAX	I'd love
HARI	Oh god I'd love
MAX	A good night's sleep.
	Pause.
MAX	The world can never be perfect that's not going to happen.
	HARI shakes his head.
MAX	But we can.
	They look at each other.
HARI	I'll get the instruction manual.
	HARI goes. MAX looks at JAN.
	HARI reappears with the manual, held open.
HARI	Here we are. There, if you get started on me then once you're done, I can do you.

MAX   Right: To boot into a basic alternative shell or
             prefabricated organism rather than launching the
             provided SKIN_GUI, you will need: a scalpel
             (sterilized), strong thread, belt or ratchet straps
             and clamps (sterilized) in addition to the provided
             BORN_setup_pack.

HARI   Right you are. I'll pop to the toolshed.

MAX   Okay. I might lay out a towel, just don't want to dirty
             the carpet.

HARI   Good idea.

MAX   Unless

HARI   What?

             Pause.

MAX   No I was just thinking

HARI   Yes perhaps you're right.

             Pause.

MAX   We're being silly aren't we?

HARI   I think I just got carried away.

MAX   That was nearly a very stupid mistake.

HARI   We should just do it in the bathroom.

MAX   Then we can wipe down the surfaces and it'll only
             take a few seconds.

HARI   I'll meet you there.

Ensuite Bathroom

Lots of blood on the floor. A bandage on HARI's head.

MAX   How do you feel?

HARI   A little queasy.

MAX	But?
HARI	Good. I feel good. Great actually.
	HARI looks at himself, feels himself, blinks in this new dawn.
HARI	Right, your turn.
MAX	Great.
HARI	Oh damnit!
MAX	What?
HARI	The spare CPU chip, it's been sitting here in the blood.
MAX	Oh bugger.
HARI	It's totally soaked.
	Pause.
HARI	I could pop to the shop.
MAX	Oh but that's a fag.
HARI	And it'll be closed at this time of night. (*He thinks.*) We could order it online?
MAX	Yes.
HARI	It'll be here tomorrow if we do it now.
MAX	Another night (*to endure*).
HARI	Hmm.
MAX	Well I suppose we don't have a choice.
HARI	Unless.
MAX	What?
HARI	Of course! I should have thought of this before. I'll pop to the attic and fish the circuit board out of that old fax machine.
MAX	Oh.

HARI	Once it's soldered onto the dry part of this should be right as rain. I knew it would come in useful.
MAX	Do you think it will be powerful enough?
HARI	Oh I'll augment it with some of the leftover pins we've still got in the pack.
MAX	Leftover
HARI	And boost the power with the battery pack from my electric toothbrush.
MAX	Right.
HARI	I should think it'll do fine. Back in a tick.
MAX	Okay, I'll wait here.

He goes. MAX is alone. She waits in silence, impassive. She picks up the instructions, looks at them, and puts them down. She picks up the toothbrush. Silence.

Ensuite Bathroom

Empty. HARI returns, holding the fax machine. He sees that the room is empty.

HARI	Max?

He looks in the bath. Not there. Pause.

HARI	Max?

Kitchen

HARI	Max?

Living Room

HARI	Darling?

Conservatory

HARI   Lovie?

Study

HARI   Love?

Teenage Boy's Bedroom

HARI   There you are. I couldn't find you anywhere.

MAX   Were you worried?

                Pause.

HARI   *(Pleased.)* No.

MAX   Not at all?

HARI   No. Just sort of… curious.

MAX   That sounds good.

                Silence.

HARI   I found the fax. It's downstairs in the bathroom.

MAX   Okay.

HARI   Shouldn't take a sec to whizz out the circuit board for you.

MAX   Great.

HARI   Shall we go then?

MAX   Yes.

                She doesn't move.

MAX   Does it feel nice?

HARI   It's wonderful actually. Plus.

MAX	Yes?
HARI	I disabled my sense of smell. So no more Wednesday night bin night worries.
MAX	That will be a relief.
HARI	And I've turned down my hearing too. So everything's just a little more
MAX	Mm?
HARI	Peaceful.
MAX	Hari?
HARI	Yes?
MAX	I don't think I want to do it. At least not tonight.
HARI	What? Why not?

MAX doesn't answer.

HARI	We can use *your* toothbrush if you'd prefer?

Pause.

HARI	We've always tried to fix things haven't we? It's a point of pride. If things are broken I don't see the harm in giving them a bit of a polish or a refit.
MAX	I suppose.
HARI	I know some people have the attitude that maybe we should all feel guilty or torture ourselves or that a bit of darkness lets you know that there's light etc. etc. I know all that. But my feeling is: wouldn't it be better if it was just always light? The fact is you only live once. And do you want to spend that time being a worry wart and moping about or would you rather get up and go and be able to enjoy things a bit more? This way is just
MAX	Nicer.
HARI	Exactly. So. Are you coming downstairs?

A long pause. MAX takes a deep breath.

MAX	Yes.

Hallway

MAX and NICK are in the hallway saying a final, awkward goodbye.

NICK   I'll see you soon okay.

MAX nods.

NICK   I'm telling you I can do this on my own.

Pause.

NICK   I'm going to do it.

MAX   You should go.

NICK   Say goodbye to Dad from me though yeah.

MAX nods. She opens the door.

NICK   It's pissing down. Fuck.

MAX   You should go.

NICK   I didn't bring a coat. Fuck.

They look at each other. NICK knows it's time to go. He reaches down for his bag.

MAX   Your finger. It's bleeding.

NICK looks at his finger.

NICK   Hardly. It's nothing.

MAX takes his hand and looks at it.

MAX   Is it sore?

NICK shakes his head. MAX stares at the tiny cut, barely visible. She strokes it with her hand and looks again at NICK. She holds the hand tight and looks again at the finger. She brings it to her lips and kisses the cut better.

MAX   There. All better.

NICK smiles.

NICK   Yeah. All better.

6

Gym

A new day, some time later. They run on treadmills.

HARI	How do you feel?
MAX	Great I feel great.
HARI	Me too.
MAX	Tired.
HARI	Me too.
MAX	But great.
HARI	Here.
MAX	Thanks.
HARI	Don't finish it though as I need to keep hydrated.
MAX	There you go.
HARI	Thanks. Looks good no?
MAX	Looks great
HARI	I knew we could get two of the cross trainers in here.
MAX	It was worth taking off the base to get them up the stairs though.
HARI	Definitely.
MAX	Otherwise we'd have struggled.
HARI	But now I think with these two in
MAX	Maybe a pull-up bar on the door
HARI	Maybe a pull-up bar on the door. And your yoga mats brought up
MAX	That would be nice.
HARI	I would say it's just about perfect.

They run and run and run.

The end.

Thanks

I'd like to thank: everyone at the Royal Court for believing in the play and working so hard to put it on; in particular Chris Campbell for getting me in in the first place and Vicky Featherstone for notes and support; Michael McCoy for pepping me up; Jenny Lee, Panda Cox, Alice Birch and my Royal Court Writers Group for feedback and thoughts; the cast and creative team for doing so much more than just following the instructions; everyone at Oberon for letting people read it; Hamish Pirie for sticking with me and taking it to another level; and Valentina for reading, supporting, noting, everything.

Inspiration

I'd like to acknowledge the influence of a few pieces of art that inspired me while I was writing *Instructions for Correct Assembly*.

Jóhann Jóhannsson's album *IBM 1401, A User's Manual*

Beautiful Boy by David Sheff

The instruction manuals of IKEA and LEGO

Teorema by Pier Paolo Pasolini

And Hari Kunzru's short story *Bodyworks*

By the same author

Pastoral
9781849434447

I'm Not Here Right Now
9781783199570

Heather
9781786822505

WWW.OBERONBOOKS.COM

Follow us on www.twitter.com/@oberonbooks
& www.facebook.com/OberonBooksLondon